THE LOONEY

AN IRISH
FANTASY

THE LOONEY
AN IRISH FANTASY

Spike Milligan

Michael Joseph
in association with Jack Hobbs
London

First published in Great Britain by Michael Joseph Ltd
27 Wrights Lane, London W8
1987
Second Impression October 1987

British Library Cataloguing in Publication Data

Milligan, Spike
The looney: an Irish fantasy.
I. Title
823'.914 [F]   PR6063.I3777
ISBN 0–7181–2870–2

Typeset by Wilmaset, Birkenhead, Wirral
Printed in Great Britain by
Billings & Sons Ltd, Worcester

I wish to dedicate this book to Paul Getty Jnr for helping support some of my causes, also to Jack Hobbs for his friendship and to Dick Douglas-Boyd for letting me call him Doug Dickless-Boyd.

NOTE

In this book I have used some characters and sketches from my ill-fated BBC series *The Melting Pot*, which for some reason beyond my comprehension was never transmitted.

THE LOONEY

In the beginning God created heaven and earth with, it would appear, Irish labour. It took the Lord six days, and on the seventh he rested, during which time speculative builders put up Kilburn. Kilburn High Street runs three miles, that's why it looks 'shagged out'. A walk through Kilburn has left an indelible blank on my mind. The British, it is said, are made up of four races, the best of these are the Derby and the Oaks.

Kilburn was a melting pot, occasionally stirred by the National Front, an extreme political organisation whose election manifesto was 'I'll punch yer fuckin' 'ead in'. The leaders were any of them that could count up to ten without having to sit down.

Kilburn High Street's once trim Victorian shopfronts were now a conjunctivitis of gaudy plastic signs whose exaggerated size suggested that the natives were in an orgy of onanism, therefore going blind. There was Nandergee Patel, Newsagent and Littlewoods Agent, Ah-Wat-Dung, Chinese Takeaway and Littlewoods Agent, Raj Curry Centre and Littlewoods Agent, and D. Smith, Funeral Directors (English Spoken) – to do business with an Englishman you had to have a death in the family.

Policemen who patrolled Kilburn had to be tranquillised before going on duty. Even the crimes were boring – drunks, petty theft and/or feeling little girls. Only that morning, had not Magistrate Mrs Thelma Skugs, who longed to be felt, given a small man three months for screwing in a doorway? 'There's far too much of this thing going on,' she had chastised him. He was dragged from the dock shouting, 'You'll never stop fucking in Kilburn.' Policemen at Kilburn Station used to kneel and pray, 'Please God, let someone get murdered tonight, preferably me!' The Lord said, 'Let the Earth bring forth grass', yea, the grass was brought forth in little packets by stoned Rastafarians. And God said, 'Be fruitful and multiply', verily every night Kilburn reverberated to the sound of shuddering bedsprings fulfilling the instructions.

In Kilburn lived a fine wreck of a man, one Mick Looney. At this moment he stood in the corner of a muddy building site that was forever England, spiteful C of E rain was falling on good Catholics. Looney was talking to himself out loud – he was deaf: 'Me farder tole me we were descended from der Kings of Catlick Oireland, so why am I standin' here in der pissin' rain mixin' cement for Mowlems?'

Even now, the torrent was turning the cement into a viscous watery soup that would one day be a floor that would fall on the heads of the tenants below.

Looney was five feet eight inches, because he hadn't gone metric. Laid on a slab his body would have invited immediate burial; he dared not fall asleep in parks for fear of people calling the Coroner. His body had never seen the sun, or for that matter the moon. Middle-aged, he had a face like a dog's bum with a hat on; two enamel blue eyes stared blankly from a DIY head.

We move now to 113b Ethel Road, a building with a slight tendency to fall down, built in Victorian days in the mock-Gothic style now mocked by everyone. Looney made 'improvements': out came those silly sash windows, in went those Ted Moult ones you 'can't hear helicopters in the garden through'. He assured his wife that 'dis will increase der price of der house', as he planted plastic tulips in the front garden . . . in December.

The building was riddled with rising damp – he had put rat traps down and caught fish. It had deathwatch beetle, dry rot, damp rot – take them away and the building wasn't there. The top floor he had 'converted' to flats, only just better than being converted to Protestantism.

This Sunday the skies above Kilburn hung with pre-natal grey clouds pregnant with chilling rain. The wife Mary and son Dick were at Mass devoutly praying, 'Please God let us

2

win Littlewoods, say £500,000.' Looney 'himself' was at home in his best suit, or the best he'd got – he had seen it in Burton's window in 1947 on a Clark Gable lookalike dummy. When Looney forced his rotund body into it it took on the appearance of a python that had swallowed a cripple. After fifteen years, his wife had donated it to 'Clothe the Ethiopian Poor' – they had sent it back with a pound.

Returning from Mass his family found him slavering over the *News of the World*: 'POP STAR'S NIGHT OF SIN IN TRANSPARENT KILT!' and 'NUDE NEGRO VICAR RUNS AMOK WITH FEATHER DUSTER!' 'PRINCE PHILIP, IS HE A TRANSVESTITE?'

He greeted his spouse, 'Ah, me darlin', how long will lunch be?'

'It should last about an hour,' she said as she slaved over a raging hell of a black stove with hellish pots issuing boiling vapour.

The food wasn't being cooked so much as tortured. Der British is terrible cooks, thought Looney, they even burnt Joan of Arc. Great jets of steam ascended upwards – after years of this there was now more nourishment in the ceiling than the food.

Looney stood to stretch his legs and collided with the washing line above. Astride his head like a jockey sat his wife's voluminous bloomers, a sexual obstacle – but for them he would have done it many more times. Grabbing the arms of the swollen imitation moquette chair he slowly lowered himself, the huge chair appeared to be devouring him. Down he went until his bum had noisily driven the last of the creaking springs to the floorboards.

He read from the *Exchange Mart & Gazette*:

Wanted, ten gallons of fish oil, will exchange for set of Indian clubs.

Twenty tins of dog food, will exchange for any Vera Lynn records or photo of the Shroud of Turin.

Old-style wooden leg, owner going abroad, will sell or exchange for Tupperware set.

3

'Ah! Here's me advert,' he said, and read aloud: 'Wanted, throne-like chair, price negotiable o.n.o. or will exchange for house-trained pure-bred mongrel, good barker, aged three but looks older o.n.o.'

A febrile o.n.o. growl with hair on came from under the table: it was Boru the pure-bred mongrel and good barker. His name had been Nigger until that Jamaican family moved in next door. Boru was old, he could now only bark lying down.

Looney glanced up at his wife, he saw the face that seen from a dead sleep would have induced a coronary, though in her young days people said she looked like a film star, Wallace Beery. She was ladling out the steaming mess called lunch.

'Oh? Wot is it?' said Looney.

'It's Sunday,' said his son.

'Are you eating, Dick?' said Mrs Looney. Whereupon Looney denied all knowledge of eating Dick.

The lad shook his head, you could hear the pieces. 'No, Mudder, I'm on a splonsored fast.'

'Splonsored? Who for?'

'Der starving Ee-thai-opeans.'

'Oh? How much do yer get?'

'I gets twenty pee for every dinner I don't eat.'

Looney himself furrowed his brow. '*Twenty pee*? Jasus! By der time youse got enough youse will be a victim yerself, man.'

'All right,' said Dick, holding out his plate.

'How long youse been doin' dis fer?' said Looney.

'Oh,' said the boy, 'three months.'

'And how much have youse saved?'

'Eighty pee.'

'God almighty. How many niggers can you feed for eighty pee?'

'About a thousand,' said Mrs Looney, walloping the steaming mess on to the plates.

They ate in silence, save the odd o.n.o. growl from Boru who could smell the food but was too old to get up.

'Now he,' said Looney, 'he'd make a fine dinner fer dem starvin' Ee-thai-opeans.'

The son winced. 'Oh no, Dad, dey wouldn't eat a doggy.'

4

Looney himself chuckled, 'Oh yes dey would! Give him a good covering of Daddy or der HP Sauce and they couldn't tell der difference.' He warmed to the argument. 'And wot about orl dose moggies dat snuff it, if dey were to put 'em in a deep-freeze ship dat would solve der hunger.' He fingered the empty bottles on the table. 'Darlin', where's der tomato sauce?'

'Most of it is in you, the rest is finished up,' said Mrs Looney. 'Hans forgot to bring any in.'

'Hans? Dat silly German bugger.'

Hans Schitz, ex-soldier taken prisoner in North Africa, had ended up on a farm in Sussex, and elected to stay on after the war to avoid travel sickness and his bank manager. Schitz couldn't stand Mrs Looney's cooking so he ate Café le Jim in Gron Street; the food was just as bad but they supplied a red goo sauce to kill the taste.

One day the supply of red goo ceased and the owner of Café le Jim, a Mister Spirious Starkios, told Schitz that the supplier of the red goo, a Mr Banarjee Tookram (BA failed) had lost his assistant through AIDS. Schitz applied for the job and soon Mr Banarjee Tookram's red goo 'Pure Tomato Sauce' was on stream again. The company was registered in Panama as an oil tanker, the red goo was stirred in a bathtub with an umbrella, syphoned into drums, then, using a syringe, squirted into plastic tomato-shaped containers for the table. Schitz brought massive quantities home to the Looneys' house – he lodged in an upstairs and terrible room where he practised boredom and onanism.

There was a whining at the back door – the Looneys' second dog Prince, named after the pop star. They daredn't let him in the house, as Looney explained to the priest: 'He's got flatulence, Fadder. Trouble is, he does dem silent butler's revenges, wid everybody in der room lookin' daggers at each udder.'

Looney went out and put a plate of Mrs Looney's food down. The dog looked at it and howled dolefully. 'Listen, mate,' said Looney, 'youse lucky youse not bein' eatin' by dem starving Ee-thai-opeans.'

He returned to his chair and observed his son. It hurt: the boy was painfully thin, he wore a second-hand suit woefully too big for him, people used to knock on it to see if he was in. He was a shy gentle boy. The Bible says, 'The meek shall inherit the earth.' Wrong, at school they beat the daylights out of him. Dick worked as a hydro boy at the Chislehurst Laundry, handling the sheets from Lewisham Hospital. Why was his son, a descendant of the Kings of Ireland, washing dem shitty English sheets? You didn't know where that shit had been.

He sat at his table checking his pools. He could be sitting on a million, instead he was sitting on currently dormant piles. 'Twenty years I bin doin' dem pools.' One day, one day . . . Some men are born losers, others have losses thrust upon them. In the human race today the Irish had come last.

THE HUNGARIAN

Frank Chezenko, one-time cavalry officer in the Austro-Hungarian forces, was now a crummy antique dealer on a hired barrow in the Portobello Road selling Art Deco toothpicks.

He looked up from *Exchange Mart & Gazette* to a large baroque Gothic chair oozing stuffing. He didn't really need it, he *did* need a good guard dog. He held his *Exchange Mart & Gazette* in a position so he could see the chair and *Exchange Mart & Gazette* at one and the same time. He then held the *Exchange Mart & Gazette* in front of the chair so he couldn't see it, then he held the *Exchange Mart & Gazette* above his head so he could see the chair without seeing the *Exchange Mart & Gazette*, he then closed his eyes so he could see neither the chair nor the *Exchange Mart & Gazette*.

When he'd left the mental home they had warned him he might suffer from eccentric behaviour. He stood and faced the mirror and saw himself naked wearing a Hussar's hat – he could see nothing wrong, he appeared to be a normal man and bloody well hung to boot. A brisk knocking on the door.

'Oo ees eet?' he shouted, placing his hat over it.

'It's me,' said a rasping voice.

My God! Mrs Ratts, his landlady! Donning an overcoat, he called, 'Come een, Mrs Ratts.'

In came a Mk V Panzer tank of a woman, breathing fire, spittle and shuddering with brown fat. She once stood on a talking weight machine. It screamed, 'Get her off!'

'The *rent*, Mr Chezenko, where is the *rent*?' A spume of hot spittle lashed Chezenko.

'Mrs Ratts, I'm afraid I'm short of ready cash.'

She shrugged her shoulders. 'Very well! You *know* our arrangement.'

7

Chezenko stood, opened his overcoat and flashed it three times.

'That's only one week!' she snapped. 'I want a month in advance!'

Flash-flash-flash . . . Chezenko flashed out his outstanding rent.

Mrs Ratts left the room with a contented smirk and Chezenko thanked God he had a landlady who still believed in barter.

Rent-free, an hour later, Chezenko put on his NHS truss and wrestled the Gothic chair into the back of his van. Slipping the gear into the only one that it would engage, he drove at 17 m.p.h. to 113b Ethel Road. As the car was dodgy, he had started early – July. With a groan he lowered the chair to the floor. After ten minutes' laughing at the house, he rang the doorbell, again and again and again he rang the doorbell, he rang it, ringed it, runged it, finally he ronged it.

After fifteen minutes, a voice spoke through the letterbox, 'Dere's a cheque in the post.'

'I come about the dog,' shouted Chezenko.

The door opened, the unshaven face of Looney peered forth, he fixed his eye on the Gothic chair. 'Is dat it?' he said.

'Yes,' said Chezenko.

'Oh,' said the Looney. 'Dat's *just* der type I'm looking for, four legs.'

'Can I see the exchange dog?' said Chezenko.

'I'll get him,' said Looney, disappearing into the house. He reappeared carrying Boru.

'What ees wrong with heem?' said the Hungarian.

'Nutting wrong, he's resting,' said Looney, laying the dog on the floor.

The Hungarian circled the creature. 'Can't he stand up?' he said.

'Oh yes,' said Looney. 'He's a good stander.'

The Hungarian whistled to the dog. 'Here, up, good boy, come on up, good boy.'

The dog didn't stir.

'Is he deaf – *yes*, deaf?' said the Hungarian.

8

'No no,' said Looney, 'he can hear mice breathing. Let *me* try. Watch dis. Come on, boy, rats, rats.' The dog didn't move.

'He's dead!' said the Hungarian.

'He's never done that before,' said Looney.

The Hungarian shook his head. 'No deal, sir,' he said, picking up the Gothic chair and backing down the path.

'No, wait,' said Looney following him. 'Let's come to some udder arrangement.'

'Yes,' said the Hungarian, 'you bury the dog and I take the chair.'

Looney wanted that chair, his heart went out to it, even his lungs, liver and kidneys. 'I got some cigarette cards of famous movie stars. Hoot Gibson, Rin-Tin-Tin, Tom Mix and all dem.'

No no no, the Hungarian could not be swayed, he backed through the gate, across the pavement and under a number 11A bus. The bus was going to Neasden, he was going to hospital. The usual crowd gathered to enjoy the accident.

'Did anyone see the accident?' said the policeman.

'Yes, I did,' groaned Chezenko from under the bus.

'His leg is broken,' said the ambulanceman.

What luck! thought Looney as he hoicked up the chair into the house. Aboard the ambulance the male nurses were struggling with a Hungarian frothing at the mouth, flashing and shouting, 'A dog! He owes me a dog!'

'Wot's dat youse got dere?' said Mrs Looney, spotting the Gothic chair.

'Ach, tis a surprise, darlin',' said Looney.

'You silly bugger,' she said, crossing herself. 'How can you surprise yerself?'

'It's not easy,' he gasped. 'Now der bad news.'

'I thought that was the bad news,' she said.

'Der dog is dead.'

'Dead,' she said unbelievingly. 'How do you know?'

Looney blinked, which for him was like taking exercise. 'He's stopped,' he said.

'He's stopped what?' she said.

9

'Everything,' he finalised, putting a TO LET sign on the kennel. The vet's prophecy had come true! He said the animal was too old to be put down: 'Leave him and he'll make it on his own.'

'Tell Dick ter get a shovel and bury him in der garden, it'll be good for der grass.'

So saying, Looney himself took the great chair into the parlour leaving a trail of stuffing. Ah! he'd soon have the chair back to its former grandeur, a good coat of gold paint with pink spots should do.

KNOLLIGE OF THE WORLD

Looney wasn't very bright at school, then he wasn't very bright at home. His parents took him to Bexhill-on-Sea; he wasn't very bright there either. They took him to Cambridge for the day; he came back none the brighter. What he needed was adult education. The answer was but a door knock away.

Ex-Sergeant Ted Philimore. After thirty years in the Buffs he retired and now, hungry and skint, he trudged his weighty suitcase of encyclopaedias to Looney's door. He wiped the sweat from his brow, down below his feet throbbed like dynamos in his shoes, and, breathing a prayer he might find a punter, he knocked on the door of 113b Ethel Road. He didn't understand why the man who answered it was wearing a false beard and moustache, which, after some questioning, he removed. Likewise, his French accent suddenly changed to Irish.

'Encyclopaedias? Wot's dem?' said Looney.

Philimore gave a knowing smile and ran his finger along his pencil-thin moustache. 'What are they? Only the knowledge of the world, that's all.' He pronounced the word 'knollige'.

'Der knollige of der world?' repeated Looney.

Philimore nodded. 'The knollige of the world,' he echoed. He used Looney's blank stare as a springboard to his next statement: 'If sirn would like a demonstration of the knollige of the world . . .' – he made the gesture of entering the home.

'Oh, sure,' said Looney, letting him only in to be called silly bugger by the parrot. This knollige of the world could be interesting – after all, that's where he lived. Looney ushered him into the parlour. Straining, Philimore hoicked the heavy suitcase on to the central table.

'Oh dat's a very good demonstration,' said Looney.

11

Philimore knew he had a soft touch. 'Oh, that isn't it, sirn, the best is yet to come,' he said. He undid a heavy-duty strap, opened the fibre case and threw back the lid, which fell off. Ignoring it, Philimore pointed to the large red volumes.

'The knollige of the world?' queried Looney.

'The knollige of the world,' repeated Philimore with great solemnity.

'Is dat all dey do?' said Looney with a pointless smile.

Philimore smiled back even more pointlessly. 'Oh no, sirn, watch this.' Like a conjuror producing a rabbit, he took one of the red volumes from the case, jumping it up and down in his cupped hand. 'Just feel the weight of that, sirn.' He handed the book to Looney who weighed the book on the palm of his hand. 'One pound eight ounces, sirn,' said Philimore. 'A very good weight for a book.'

The two great minds stood looking at each other.

'May I?' said Philimore, reaching for the book.

'Oh, yes,' agreed Looney.

Philimore, with a superior smile, keeping his eye on the hypnotised Looney, flipped open the book. With the anima of Jesus doing the loaves and fishes, he ran a finger down the page. 'Listen to this, sirn . . .' At this stage it would be wise to inform the reader that Mr Philimore knew nothing about the encyclopaedia. His one-hour crash sales course consisted of 'Sell it or you get bugger all'. He read from the page, 'The Hanging Gardens of Babylon, 3000 BC.' He looked up like he had just invented penicillin.

'Is dat right?' said Looney.

'The knollige of the world, sirn,' said Philimore. 'Don't go, here's another.' He read again, 'The Nilgiri Hills, tea-growing area of the west coast of India.'

Looney gasped, this was stuff he didn't know about, this was what posh people knew. They could walk into a room and say, Hello Jim, the Nilgiri Hills, tea-growing area in west India, yes, was there more?

'Would sirn like to try?' said Philimore, now faint with hunger. Looney took the book. 'Go on, sirn, open it at random.'

12

Looney leafed through the pages, R-R-R-R-, ah, here it was, Random . . . haphazard, without purpose.

'It's a book that can give you a large portion of knollige, sirn,' said Philimore. 'For instance, say you were at a party at the American Hembassy and someone said [and here he put on an appalling American accent], "Say, buddy, do you know Abraham Lincoln's Gettysburg Address," what would sirn say?'

Looney said he didn't know it, surely care of the White House, Washington, would get him?

Philimore went on, staggering Looney with information: the giant squid was sixty foot long, the thylacine was extinct in Tasmania, Newgrange was the largest monolith stone grave in the world. Gradually he was breaking Looney down by sheer salesmanship, but what finally broke Looney was when Philimore fell on his knees, clutched Looney round the legs, burst into tears, showed him a picture of his wife and kids, his war medals, his rates demand and an unpaid bill for groceries, throwing in at the last minute that he too was Roman Catholic, ending up with, 'Fer Christ's sake, buy a set. I'm fucking starvin'.'

Looney signed the HP agreement for monthly payments over the next sixteen years and paid a five-pound deposit, whereupon Mr Philimore fainted. After cooking him two eggs, bacon and chips the revived salesman left with a five-pound note and tears in his eyes, both fakes.

THE BURIAL

That night, stiff as a board, they buried the dog four legs upwards.

Mrs Aida Higgs, the aged short-sighted next-door neighbour, heard the nocturnal digging. In the gloom she espied the outline of the Looneys burying 'something' in the garden. Brought up on the *Sun*'s shock-horror journalism, she dialled 999. 'There's something strange going on in the next-door garden.'

Constable Albert Ward rang the bell on 113b Ethel Road.

'Dere's a cheque in der post,' hissed a voice through the letterbox.

'Excuse me,' said the constable addressing the letterbox, 'it's the Police, we'd like a word with the owner.'

There was a pause, the letterbox said, 'Wot television set, officer?' and went on, 'Der's no television set in here.'

During this time, Mrs Looney was covering it with a white altar cloth placing a crucifix atop. When Constable Ward was admitted, Mrs Looney and son Dick were kneeling and praying before it, the ten o'clock news issuing from it escaping the constable's notice. The constable would like to examine the garden. 'Oh, dat's paid for as well,' said sweating Looney. The constable observed the newly disturbed earth: either the victim was a dwarf or they had buried him doubled up.

'How many people live here?' he said.

'All of us,' said Looney.

The constable inspected the garden, sensing he was on the verge of a great murder discovery. Scraping the surface, he came across four paws. 'Yes, der dog he's buried dere. You're standin' on his head.' Constable Ward returned to duty, two Valiums and *Playboy*.

THE HINDUS

Sandwich was a long way from Frank Chezenko's accident, and this morning a curtain of sea-fret cloaked the coastline. The sea was limp and tea-tray flat, grounded seagulls waited for flying weather.

From out of the misted haunted sea came the creaking sound of badly maintained rowlocks and the grunting of a badly maintained human. Occasionally came a burst of Hindu voices – it all sounded like a very difficult clue in the *Times* crossword. The Hindu chatter was suddenly silenced by a gruff, 'Fer fuck's sake, keep it dahn.' A rowboat loomed into view like an emerging embryo, three shadowy figures crouched above the gunnels. Its prow sliced into the sand, then, like a dog's tongue, lolled to one side. A seaman with a cap, a broken nose and a small overdraft leapt out and pulled the vessel further in. The two Hindu passengers stood wobbling on jelly legs, they passed the seaman their suitcases. Carefully he threw them on to the beach where they split open like gaping oysters. 'Oh dear,' said the seaman, 'the damp has melted the cardboard.'

The two passengers were father and son, Bapu and Percy Lalkaka, last forwarding address c/o The Gutter, Calcutta. They had escaped from the grinding poverty of India to the grinding poverty of England. They re-stuffed their suitcases and re-tied the string.

'That'll be two 'undred pahnds,' said the seaman's out-stretched hand.

From a roll of money the bearded elder Hindu counted out the amount, while the younger strained his eyes inland. 'Is this the place?' he said.

The seaman nodded, 'Yer.'

15

'This is *London*?'

'The outskirts.'

'Vere are all the London people?'

'It's early closin', innit?'

'Vere is the transport you promised?'

'Ah! You walks up that way an' you'll come to a big road, lots of lorries and cars goin' by. You hold up yer thumb like this and make this signal, and when one stops that's the one who knows the secret.' So saying, his shoulders heaving with suppressed laughter, he rowed back into the mist, collided with a drifter and sank, his floundering cries for help misconstrued by the Hindus as some nautical term used in mists.

Picking up their luggage they made for the motorway. In their possession they had personal letters of introduction to one of England's 'leading' housing agents, a Mr Looney, and another letter to Bernie Gilstein the Home Secretary, who would meet them any Wednesday in Frith Street outside Ronnie Scott's Club where he would arrange for them to get passports and British citizenship and a blue movie video, all for five pounds cash.

THE PHONE-IN

Looney pondered – this paralysed the rest of his body, something was fretting at the smooth surface of his delinquent mind. Was he *really* descended from the Kings of Ireland? His father *had* said so on his HP deathbed, he swore Mick to silence otherwise they would have to pay death duties and VAT on the royal estate, consisting of a derelict cottage and a sack of potatoes that were older than the sack of Rome. The spuds were eaten at the wake and the cottage fell down during a fit of coughing.

This night the inheritor of that royal estate sat up in bed eating Smith's onion-flavoured crisps, Maltesers and Watney's Export Ale. 'If dis is fer export, what's it doin' in this country?' Next to him Mrs Looney read the *Sun* and ate a pork pie; she would have been better nourished and better read had she eaten the *Sun* and read the pie. Looney knelt by the bed his head bowed.

'Are you prayin'?' said his wife.

'No, I'm havin' a piss,' he said. This very po had belonged to his grandfather. Every time he used it he recalled the dear man, how proud he would have been.

On a bedside table that owed its existence to UHU, an early Japanese transistor was grinding out a late-night phone-in: idiots who pay for the phone call fill up the stations' timetable free of charge while a partially informed DJ sits in judgement.

Right now a toothless crone was saying, 'I don't fink sex is free anough in this country, we should be able to get it on the National 'Ealth.'

Ah! thought Looney, I'll ask dis dish jockey. Holding the innards of the phone in its container, he dialled the number.

Soon he was in the queue with a thousand other unpaid entertainers.

Eventually, 'Hello, it's midnight,' said the DJ [Big Deal!], 'This is Crapitol Radio, you are listening to 'Talk Box' with Tom Lengths. Now we have a Mr Loney of Kilburn, hello Mr Loney of Kilburn.'

'No, it's not Loney, I'm Looney.'

'Ha ha, aren't we all?' said the pain in the arse. 'Ha ha ha, but seriously, Mr Looney, what is your question?'

'I want to, hello? Hello? Tom?'

'Ha ha, yes we're still here Mr Looney.'

'How can I find out about me ancestors, like?'

'Ha ha, yes, there's *Burke's Peerage*, quite a few berks there, ha ha ha, and the Public Records Office,' said the pain in the arse. 'Now we take a break now.'

Looney heard a burst of amnesia-inducing music, then, 'Brentford Nylons! Grand Sale on *now*, prices slashed, sheets from 20p to fifteen hundred pounds.' 'Hello? Hello?' Looney hung up. Why was this dish jockey suddenly trying to sell him Brentford Nylons?

He must make a note of dem names. 'Darlin', has youse got a pencil?'

'Yes, if youse go downstairs in the kitchen dere's one on a bit of string.'

Never mind, he could remember it, *Bronks Peerage* and the Record of Public Offices, that was easy to remember, yes, *Brons Peerage* and the Record of Public Orifices.

A squawky voice came wafting up the stairs: 'Who's a pretty boy? . . . you silly bugger . . . who's a pretty boy?'

Looney sat up. 'It's der bloody parrot! Did you not put his cover on?'

Wearily Mrs Looney rose from the matrimonial bed and descended the stairs.

'Can you bring der pencil back wid youse?' he shouted.

'You silly bugger, awk you silly bugger' wafted up the stairs.

Mrs Looney returned with a pencil and a bitten finger. Looney wrote down, Briggs Peerage and Richard of Punic Artifices.

18

Like a dental *pas de deux* the Looneys removed their teeth, and, synchronised, dropped them into glasses of water where they magnified into great effervescent Steradent grins. Mrs Looney intoned gummy prayers over her rosary: 'Please God, £500,000, remember.' Himself turned his bedside lamp off, turned on his side and thought, Now where's dat Sophia Loren . . . ?

THE ENCOUNTER

By mid-morning the sea-fret mist over the coast of Sandwich had risen, as had Constable Ken Krench. He had just finished his first morning 'enquiry', a Mrs Nardia Thrills who was always available for questioning the moment her husband left for the jam factory. Now, after the sexual manipulations of Mrs Thrills, he puffed and perspired as he cycled up El Alamein Street, while at home Mrs Thrills was musing over the policeman's foreplay, that had consisted of 'Ello darlin', look at this!' which was better than her Jewish husband's, which was twenty minutes of begging and a post-dated cheque.

Blinking, Krench spotted what appeared to be two suspicious 'darkies' carrying suitcases coming from the beach. 'Bloody wogs! They shouldn't be in a white man's country, they should stay where the curry is, comin' over here giving decent people the shits and smallpox.' He dismounted as they approached. 'Excuse me, gentlemen' – he got no further, the elder of the two wogs spoke, 'Good morning, constable of old England, how are we? Good health! My son and I are tourists on holiday from Amsterdam.'

Constable Krench paused – he wasn't the brightest of men and pauses helped him – Amsterdam? He scrambled the word in his head, Dmasmater . . . Ertsmadma . . . Stermadam . . . Matsmaerd . . . No, it was no good, he didn't know what an Amsterdam was. 'Er have you any means of identification?' Ah, Bapu Lalkaka knew *exactly* what to do, had not the boatman given him the secret? Carefully he peeled off ten one-pound notes. 'There you are, constable, sir.'

Krench blinked. 'Ah, yes sir, these papers appear to be in order. Good-day, gentlemen, have a nice holiday.' He swung

20

his leg over his bike, crushed his balls and crashed down screaming on the other side. 'Are you in pain?' said Bapu.

'Fuck off,' said the constable, who now knew that policemen's trousers, like all GLC buildings, have no ballroom.

Pantechnicon after pantechnicon, car after car, slushed by, drenching the two frantically thumbing Hindus.

'He is a long time in coming,' said the rain-decked Percy, the water settling like a pond in the dent in his trilby.

'Patience, my son,' said Bapu, well on his way to bronchitis, 'the Henglish never break their word, they'll break your bloody neck but never their word.'

A giant road-crushing pantechnicon bearing German trade plates pulled to a hissing Wagnerian hydraulic halt, the logo on its side said

'Von Eidelberger's Cornish Pasties, Like Mum Makes'

The cab door opened to reveal a Zulu in overalls. 'Vere are you goink, meiner friends?' he said in a clipped German accent.

'We are goink to London's well-known Frith Street.'

'Zis is your lucky day,' he said to the rain-soaked Hindus, 'I am goink right past it.' He did look past it.

Gratefully the Hindus, who were both past it themselves, ascended the cab. In the heated interior the sopping Hindus started to steam, causing unending condensation.

'Stop zat,' said the frantic German spade trying to clean the windscreen.

'You recognised the secret sign,' said Percy, indicating his thumb.

'Ya,' said the driver. 'Ha ha, ve *all* recognise zat.'

Bapu was pondering the black driver – ex-Nazis would do anything to disguise themselves. 'Pardon, me but are you Henglish?'

The driver shook his head. 'Nein, hi ham German, zer Vest German Republic, my name is Hans Von Mugabe.'

21

Bapu grinned, a good thing to do when totally baffled. 'Ve are from Amsterdam, ve are coming to see the Duke of Buckingham Palace, the Tower Blocks of London and the Housing of Parliament.'

The Zulu grinned, a good thing to do when baffled.

The motion of the journey and the heat of the cab lulled the Hindus into a deep steaming Vindaloo sleep.

Back in Sandwich Constable Krench lay in a hospital bed, his balls now bright blue and five times their normal size resting on a trestle to take the weight. Mrs Thrills would have a restful week, and a post-dated cheque.

THE HINDUS II

London! Steaming metropolis of grot, grime, grit, gunk and gunge, mugging, Molotov cocktails, rape, football hooligans, bombs and assassinations. Dr Johnson said, 'He who is tired of London is tired of life' – fuck him. Faceless monstrous buildings thrust mindless and screaming up to the sky, a style known as Art Leggo. Buildings that, because of their sterility, denied the artisan work, the woodcarver, the marble and stone mason, the marquetry expert, the brass inlayer, the iron-craft master, the plaster moulder – all now lost in the four million unemployed. Architecture was dead, construction was in, slot square A into slot B continue upwards and voilà! An enclosed space with glass. Classic London squares systematically ruined – vistas of St Paul's blocked out. The cause of conservation is only *just* alive. How can there be any strength in depth when one day Michael Heseltine is Secretary for the Environment, his task to conserve, next he is Minister for War, whose job it is to destroy, next, he's not a minister at all! A big laugh. Even the heir apparent, who can't stand what they are doing and speaks out, he won't stop it. Even as he speaks the Seifert clan are designing a monstrous edifice that will destroy and dwarf the Limehouse area. The conscience of the nation is made up of money and money alone, it seems the whole city exists on a tightrope of finance, a dollar drop in the price of oil and the brokers swallow Valium and shit themselves. Jesus, is this the lot you died for? The young innocent and the confused take to drugs and end up in asylums. This is the city that will welcome the Lalkakas. At this moment they were being awakened from their betel-nutted dreams.

'Vake up, Dutchmen.' Von Mugabe was shaking Bapu.

'Oh, vere are ve?'

'Just here hi am droppink you, it is zer Cambridge Circus, zer Frith Street is up zere.'

Wearily the two tired passengers lowered themselves on to even tireder pavements.

Ronnie Scott once said that Frith Street raised the tone of the gutter, 'We're getting a better class of mugger.' Crime existed on an exquisite scale and perverts proliferated. Only the previous night Len Toley the silversmith and his wife were watching the repeat of the repeat of *Dynasty* when they were interrupted by the doorbell. He was greeted at the door by two vicars wearing stocking masks. There was an awkward silence.

' 'Oo are you?' said Mr Toley. One vicar stepped forward. 'We are Jehovah's Burglars,' he said.

'I don't understand,' said Mr Toley.

'You see,' the man went on, 'we are being persecuted by the Police for our beliefs.'

'Oh,' queried Mr Toley. 'What are your beliefs?'

'We believe,' said the man, pushing Mr Toley back into the hall, 'that you've got a lot of silver in the house.'

Mr Toley remembered the floor coming up to meet him. The vicars tippy-toed into the front room. Mrs Toley sat with her back to the door, which was better than back to the dole. 'That you, Len? You've missed the bit where JR is 'avin' it away with –' She stopped as the blackjack did to her what Toley would loved to have done years ago. When they came to, the silver had gone, but worse! *Dynasty* had finished.

Hungry now, the two Hindus vectored in on a promising shop, HAMBURGERS, ah yes! This was the cheap fast food, wrong! This was *Lew* Hamburgers, betting shop. Down sodden steps into a desperate room anointed with poverty went the hungry pair. Stepping over a drunken punter stretched out on the floor, they approached a counter and addressed Australian Bill Kerr, a policeman dismissed by the Brisbane Police for taking bribes but never sharing them out.

'Excuse me, sir,' said Bapu, 'vot do you recommend?'

24

The Australian looked up from the betting slips to the race board behind him. 'Well, the popular favourite is Herpes Hal.'

'Very well, we'll have two.'

'Two?' the Aussie queried. 'There's only one Herpes Hal.'

'All right, we'll have one between the two of us.'

'You want it each way?'

'Ve'll have it *anyway*.'

The Australian started to make the betting slip out: 'Herpes Hal, ten to four.'

'Pardon me,' said Bapu, 'we are strangers in this country of yours, vot exactly is a Herpes Hal?'

Bloody Abos! 'It's a horse, mate.'

The Hindus were thunderstruck. 'Horse?' said Bapu.

'Yes, there.' The Australian pointed to the board. 'Two-year-old stakes.'

'Vot?' said Bapu. 'You are selling us two-year-old Herpes Hal steaks made from horsemeat, and you want us to wait till ten to four for them? Ve will be dead from starvation by then. Come, Percy.' So saying, the sons of India took their hunger elsewhere.

THE SEARCH

Looney and son Dick entered the portals of the Public Records Office. He in his Clark Gable suit, Dick in that huge Oxfam one that made him look like one of the victims. The place was highly organised: the commissionaire on the ground floor sent them to Room 34b on the first floor, who redirected them to Room 119 on the third. They in turn sent them to Room 2334 on the fifth floor, who kindly directed them to Room 2 on the fourth floor, who helpfully redirected them back to the commissionaire on the ground floor now at lunch on the sixth floor.

'Fuck dis,' said Looney, wandering sheeplike along the faceless corridors.

A passing faceless corridor clerk took pity. 'Can I help you?' she said.

Looney shrugged. 'I don't know, can you?'

'What is it you're looking for?'

'I'm looking fer dat bloody commissionaire,' said Looney with threatening fist.

'What exactly is it you want?' she said.

'We want der birts, debts and miscarriages.'

She pointed down the corridor. 'That door at the end.'

Grunting their thanks, the Looney duo presented themselves at a desk next to a small button with the notices 'Ring For Attention' and 'Out of Order'. It was a large room rampant with desks, at which hunched people pored over large volumes, all trying to unlock some past secret. From a door appeared a middle-aged female wearing a nylon dustcoat – she had a face that a myopic child of four would have made out of Plasticine and balanced on her microcephalic head was a blue-rinse-laquered 'hairdo'. Surely this was the face that invented the custard pie? Mid-face were a set of huge National Health Service dentures which looked like Stonehenge.

'You 'ave ter fill in this card first,' said the teeth.

'Oh,' pondered Looney. 'Yer see, I can't write.'

'You illiterate?'

'I can read a bit, I can't write.'

'Sort of semi-literate?'

'Dat'll do, put dat down fer me.'

''Ow do you spell yer name?'

'I don't.'

'Well *say* it.'

'Looney.'

'What, like in bin?'

'Bin?'

'Yes, looney bin.'

'I never been in der bin.'

'I meant *spelt* like looney bin.'

'Yes.'

'Age.'

'I tink I'm fifty.'

'Don't you know?'

'No, but I feels fifty.'

'You look older . . . sixty.'

'All right, put down feels fifty but looks sixty.'

Carefully the teeth took down the details, as a lone fly landed on her ear bringing her a touch of glamour. 'Do you know the date of your birth?'

'Oh yes,' said Looney, with great confidence.

They stood staring at each other. 'Well?' She was rapidly losing her temper, her looks and her figure.

'Well what?' said Looney.

'What's the date of your birth?'

'Ohhhhhh *dat*,' said Looney. 'It was the Turd of July 1928.'

She departed and returned with the requisite volume. For months every weekend and every weekend for months, Looney scoured the Public Records but found no trace of royal blood, not even by transfusion. It did show that back as far as records went his family were labourers called X from Drool in

27

Donegal. What a coincidence, his brother lived there! The search *must* go on.

'Dear Your Majesty the Queen, Can you tell me if there are any Looneys on your side of the family?' The Queen's secretary replied in the negative. 'She might be lyin',' said Looney. 'She wants ter keep it all fer herself and dat Bubble and Squeak.'

THE CHURCHILL SUITE

Bapu explained to a pair of framed suspicious red eyes in a letterbox that they had a letter of introduction from their boatman Admiral Styles. This caused the door to open.

'Oh yes,' said Looney. 'Oh yes, youse is der two fellers from Asthmadam.' He winked.

'Who is it?' wailed Mrs Looney's voice.

'It's dem two wogs,' hissed Looney. 'Follow me, fellas,' he said, ascending the stairs. Halfway up, he paused. 'Youse know I like one month's rent in advance.' The Lalkakas smiled and nodded. 'Silly old bugger' came the cry from below. 'Take no notice,' said Looney. 'Dat's der parrot.' 'Shut up, bastard' came a second cry. 'Take no notice, dat's der wife.'

On the landing they passed a Chinaman cooking on a gas stove with two Arabs queuing up behind him. The next flight was flanked by purple flock wallpaper with a lone evil painting of what was intended to be Jesus issuing forth from the tomb, but could be construed as a mongoloid who had just butted his way through a stone wall. 'Me son painted dat, never had a day's trainin'.' The top landing had a further gas stove.

'Dis is yours,' said Looney, proudly opening a door into a dank gloom-laden attic – the walls had been painted doom grey to which had been added little cheerful red spots. 'Like it?' he beamed. 'I done it meself, I calls it der Churchill Suite.'

The Lalkakas gazed round at the grim interior with a view of the brick wall through the window. 'When youse cleaned dem windows youse will be able to see dat brick wall much clearer.' Looney pointed to above the fireplace, where

29

was nailed an old newspaper cut-out of Gandhi, who was never cut out for newspapers.

'Gandhi,' said Looney. 'Youse all heard of Gandhi.'

'Not lately,' said Percy.

'All very interesting,' said Bapu. 'Now, can ve see our room?'

Looney pursed his lips. 'Dis *is* der room.'

Percy took one pace forward, a thing unheard of in the confines of Calcutta. 'Ve were promised first-class accommodation, this is crappy.'

Looney straightened his shoulders. 'Yes, dis is first-class crappy accommodation. Don't youse know dere's a financial squeeze on?'

'Oh yes,' said Percy. 'And this is one of them. How are ve going to keep warm?'

'Can't you eat a curry?' countered Looney.

No, they wanted heating.

'I'll send der dog up, he gives off a lot of heat.'

'Send the *dog* up? Do you think we are bloody fools?'

'Unless my information was faulty.'

'Ven we say heating we mean solid fuel fireplaces, that or oil or gas central heating, failing which, three-kilowatt blow-heaters, thus keeping the room at a steady twenty-four degrees centigrade or seventy-six degrees fahrenheit. A dog does not radiate sufficient heat: the body hairs of a dog are trapped in the follicles, preventing heat loss which is why dogs in the Northern hemisphere have long coats – like Huskies – whereas dogs in tropical climates have short hair, or as in the case of Mexican dogs, they are bald.'

Looney was baffled: he was bald and he had *never* been near Mexico.

'My father and I are not concerned as to whether your head has never been to Mexico. If ve accept this accommodation ve want heating other than a dog or a curry.'

Looney growled. This is what bloody education did! 'All right, I'll get youse a heater,' he said. 'Now it's tirty pounds a week.'

Bapu Lalkaka crashed to the floor clutching his chest.

30

Looney knelt by his side. 'Is it yer heart?' he said. 'No, the price.'

After three hours' protracted argument he finally gave in. 'All right! Six pounds a week and a month in advance.' His beady eyes lasered on to the money as it was counted into his Girobank hands.

'Ve would like a receipt,' said Bapu.

'Oh no!' laughed Looney. 'Dere's no need fer dat, I trust you.' He backed from the room like a gunman.

They could hear him counting and recounting the money as he descended the stairs, each time arriving at a different total. The Lalkakas inspected the bed bunks.

'Vy one up and one down?' said Percy.

'It is because of the upper and lower classes. If a wild beast gets in, it eats the lower class, leaving the upper class safe and sound.'

How, thought Looney, had the Lalkakas come by the money? In the dark desperate days at the beginning of the war England had promised India her freedom if she would help England out of the trouble which she was up to her neck in. Gandhi had agreed and while India mobilised they tried to help England's cigarette shortage. Indian scientists claimed that given sufficient funds they could make V for Victory cigarettes out of cow shit, Churchill sent half a million pounds, and then work started. Then a demand for more funds, another half million was sent. This was repeated three more times.

Finally Churchill spoke to Gandhi by phone. 'Gandhi,' said the great man, 'what is the hold up? It's been eighteen months.'

Well, sir,' Gandhi explained, 'everything is fine. They look like cigarettes, they taste like cigarettes, but they still smell like shit.'

Both Percy and Bapu had worked at the factory as sweepers, being Harijan untouchables, but as the war went on this was overlooked: Bapu joined the army and was with General Montgomery; Percy did better, he was with General

31

Electric. They lived frugally and saved every penny. Bapu's wife too was on war work on a building site. Alas, she died from deafness – there was a steamroller coming up behind her, they buried her in an envelope. The company paid Bapu compensation, at last! His marriage had paid off!

The war was over and, apart from Elliott Ness, the Untouchables became a despised class again. This the Lalkakas exploited, they took to begging in the streets threatening to touch any high-class Hindu who didn't pay them. When he needed a break Bapu would lie outside Sister Theresa's Hospice for the dying feigning the plague. After five weeks' devoted nursing and food he would return to begging, where his son on a wooden cart was pretending to be a cripple. With a reasonable bank balance they had returned to their smallholding outside Poona; when funds ran low, they took to the streets again. News came through of the rich pickings available in England and of how successful Hindus and Pakistanis called Patel were in London. The Lalkakas entered England through the German-Dutch underground, now more crowded than the London Underground. Now they were in the attic of 113b Ethel Road: one thing for sure, it was better than the gutter in Calcutta, but only just.

THE EXPOSURE

Chezenko, in pain with a fractured ankle and wrist, trying to tell medics he'd been robbed of his Gothic chair and minus a dog, was inserted like a suppository into the ambulance. 'You'll be all right,' said a stout nurse. All right? He'd *never* been all right, he'd been a flasher from birth.

Born in Budapest before the Russians came, he had flashed at a time when Hungary was romantic, with wild Zingaro music in the cafés. Yes, he had flashed to many Romany tunes, no ordinary exposures, he had flashed at some of the highest in the land. A picture of his willy was on the Hungarian State Police record books; yes, he had done light prison sentences, but on his release had not the Countess Zena Baritsh actually thrown a party for him to flash at, ah? The applause was still ringing in his ears. Then came that terrible day with the Russian tanks, and he swore a solemn oath that a Russian woman would never *never* see him flash, a true patriot. For a while he only flashed 'underground', but a Russian spy informed on him and soon he was in the custody of the dreaded AVO! They took him into custody, twisted his willy and stamped it TILOS* in red letters, ruined! His hobby was ruined! He must escape the repressive red regime. England! That's where he'd go. Using the secret underground, he flashed his way to freedom. Ah! what a tolerant country, they had legalised homosexuality, gays and lesbians no longer needed to go unrecognised, it was all legal, the day could not be far off when flashers too would get their freedom. Perhaps one might have a licence.

* Censored.

33

GLC LICENCE   NO:28

**THIS MAN IS ALLOWED TO FLASH OFFICIALLY FROM
12TH NOVEMBER UNTIL DECEMBER 24TH
BETWEEN QUEENSWAY AND MARBLE ARCH STATIONS.**

SIGNED

Ken Livingstone

All this went through his head as he lay recovering in the Kilburn Royal Hospital. What excellent NHS service he'd been given, the kindness of the nurses. He had gone in with a sprained wrist and ankle with hair fractures. To ease the pain in the ambulance they had put him to sleep with Pentathol, oh, the delicious feeling and those delightful anaesthetic dreams . . .

The orchestra played an uptempo swinging version of Cole Porter's 'Just One of Those Things' and a voice announced, 'It's nine o'clock live from the stage of the London Palladium. We present Flasher of the Year.' The applause burst like a thunder, led by a claque leader, as on to the stage came Michael Parkinson.

'Good evening and welcome to Flasher of the Year. Tonight the jury have considered the three winning contestants, and here in reverse order are the winners: in third place, from Hackney Wick, apprentice plumber, no relation to Christopher, ha ha, Warren Harvey!' Down the gold-spangled steps appeared the lucky man in full evening dress, top hat and a satin cape. Walking down he flashed at each step while the commentator carried a message to the TV millions. 'Warren Harvey, vital statistics five and a quarter inches, a light pink colour.' The audience applauded. Solemnly Parkinson handed him 'A holiday for one, three weeks all-paid in Scunthorpe!'

There followed the second prize: 'Four and a half inches, brown with slight abrasions, Derek Lambert from Shepherds Bush wins a candlelit supper with Mary Whitehouse.' Then there was Frank Chezenko! In the full uniform of a Hungarian Hussar, cloaked in a great cavalry overcoat. 'The outright winner, with seven inches and bluish pink veins who wins the Golden Raincoat, and the waist-high practice mirror, Frank Chezenko!'

... Yes, Pentathol, what a pity it's not on prescription. Another pity, when he regained consciousness: he'd been operated on for piles. Four weeks he hadn't been able to walk and had to sleep standing up, but now, discharged and recovering, there was another thing he wanted to recover – the Gothic chair. That Irishman wasn't going to get away with it.

THE DREAMER

Looney searched the larder for a TV snack. Three damp Brooke Bond teabags ready for re-use, a slice of white bread with green spots on which was starting to look like a Joan Miró painting, a tin of sardines swimming in oil, no wonder they drowned, a plastic box with a film of margarine, as films go it was better than some on TV. Ah, this is it, the half-eaten corpse of a Kentucky Fried Chicken, last re-fried by a Lebanese in Kilburn. He kicked the TV alive, settled himself back in his Gothic throne, and, munching the dead body, he sipped Watneys bladder-crippling beer, sucked at a king-size cigarette that gave you king-sized cancer, with his feet on a stool as he viewed the screen. There was something erotic about seeing Joan Collins's face between a pair of feet – he put his toe under her nose and guffawed, he played the field pressing the buttons on the remote control: *Dynasty* to *Brookside*, *Police Five*, *Nine O'Clock News*, *Wogan*, what's dis? Huge Wheldon doin' *Royal Heritage*, der Coronation of George the Turd . . .

what a coronation procession his would be! on each side of kilburn high street would be solid gold cement-mixers studded with pearls. bricklayers in white satin overalls would form an arch of silver trowels flicking pink cement. the route would be lined with navvies presenting arms with spangled pickaxes. he'd wear a tousand-pound suit and a superman cloak with shamrocks. he and the queen would arrive by guinness lorry driven by the cardinal from 'the thorn birds'. bob geldof and the boomtown rats in kilts would play 'danny boy'.

when they arrived at 113b ethel road the door would be opened by the manager of harrod's food hall. a roll of red lino would come out. in the front room he would sit on the gothic throne chair. his wife on the sofa. paddy malone and the chieftains would play 'ave maria means i love you'. in a neutral corner pope john paul

would say 'I pronounce you king of Ireland.' the chairman of
mowlems would kiss his boots and say, 'king looney, we're going ter
give you another three pounds a week and you needn't come to
work till nine-thirty.' the king would make a statement: 'the
hanging gardens of babylon – 3000 BC.' then dominic behan the poet
laureate would give the royal address, 'one hundred and tirteen
B ethel road', and they would all cheer. then he would switch the
gold television on and watch a command performance of the 'gay
byrne show' repeat...

THE RETURN VISIT

Chezenko hobbled up the door (hobbling doors was another of his perversions), he knocked with his plaster-covered hand – he didn't have to wait long.

'Dere's a cheque in der post,' said the letterbox.

Chezenko shouted back angrily, 'I come to recover my chair.'

'Dat's very nice of you,' said Looney, 'but I've already recovered it.'

Angrily Chezenko hammered on the door breaking his plaster. Under the assault Looney opened the door.

'I want the chair back,' said Chezenko.

'Only the back?' stalled Looney. 'I got annuder fine dog, fine barker.'

Chezenko smirked – not a bad smirk for a non-smirker. 'Is it *alive*?'

Looney nodded. 'I'll get him.' He produced Prince the flatulencing canine during a fallow period. Chezenko circumnavigated the dog, he examined all his parts, looked in his ears, teeth – yes, this one seemed to be working.

'All right,' said Chezenko.

Looney handed him the string. Now the big one!

'Where's my van?' Chezenko said.

'Oh! dat's safe, I parked it round the back. I'll show youse.' Yes, there it was, safe round the back, FOR SALE £100. 'Just a joke,' said Looney, tearing it off, but then he was always tearing them off.

Stuffing the dog in the back, Chezenko drove off at 17 m.p.h. to a nightmare journey. Prince let go six Butler's Revenges in the small confines, nearly asphyxiating the Hungarian. Hanging out of the window, he turned the van round and at 17½ m.p.h. headed back.

'I'm sorry about der dog fartin',' said Looney.

'*You're* sorry,' said the Hungarian.

'Let's come to some udder arrangement,' said Looney.

'Yes,' said the Hungarian. 'You give me three pounds, that's the arrangement!'

'Three pounds!' gasped Looney and went giddy.

'Yes, three pounds or I'll send the boys round.'

Oh, couldn't he send the girls? *Three pounds*, it was driving a hard bargain, but Looney too drove a hard bargain – right now it was parked in a side street.

Both men argued the price, both Looney and both Chezenko both boths finally settled on two pounds and a set of famous film star cigarette cards. Looney went to rub his hands together and missed. At last! the Gothic throne chair was his.

In the kitchen Mrs Looney was ironing the Pretender to the Irish Throne's vest, steering the iron around the holes like a slalom.

'Der trone chair is mine,' he joyfully told her as her cigarette ash burnt yet another hole in the garment.

'How do youse know your father was tellin' the truth?' she said.

'I heard it from his own lips,' said Looney. 'A man wouldn't lie on his death bed.'

'Well, he had to lie on something,' she said.

'No,' said Looney. 'Dere's lots of pretenders to der throne: France, Germany, Portugal, Gibraltar, Malta.'

Yes, he too could pretend as good as them. Painting that Gothic chair gold had been a good start. He felt regal sitting in it, despite the springs sticking up his bum, therefore he mostly stood by it. He had set it up facing the television, a Pretender had to be informed what was going on in the world: *Dallas*, *Dynasty*, *Eastenders*, the testcard, all those things.

'I finished, Dad,' said Dick, holding up the homemade CD plate on a piece of cardboard.

Ah! This would put an end to parking fines!

THE TRAFFIC WARDEN

No, not all those bemedalled veterans carrying banners past the Cenotaph were heroes. Many didn't volunteer, most were conscripted, many spent the war racking their brains how to get out. Eating soup to fibrillate the heart, stuffing cushions up their backs saying they were deformed, pretending they were deaf, dumb, daft, making chicken noises when spoken to, putting shaving foam in their mouths and barking, feigning rabies. Suddenly the war was over. They *were* the victors! Medals were distributed to those who hadn't even heard a gun go bang, anyone in uniform was adulated, they were heroes!

One of these was Len Gollops. At his medical he appeared with bare feet, leapt on to the interview table and started to eat the *Daily Mirror*. Members of the Board watched in silence until he had finished, the Medical Officer said, 'Very good, you're the tenth newspaper eater we've had this morning', and passed him A1 with the recommendation 'very fine actor'.

He was sent to the Pioneer Corps, but he still tried, coming on parade naked howling like a wolf. It wasn't wasted on his sergeant who said, 'Stop actin' like a cunt.' Clucking like a chicken, he was posted overseas: Alderney! When the Germans invaded he suddenly stopped clucking – mainly because they beat the living daylights out of him. 'Lay eggs or stop zat,' they had warned. After the war he had told people that he took to the 'hills' of Alderney and became a Resistance leader called 'The Black Terror', whereas his record showed he became a POW and ended up as a sluice operator on a Nazi sewage farm in Dortmund.

How he envied the power of those prison camp Kapos. 'Pick up zat shit,' they'd say and he'd have to do it. He told them he had been a member of Oswald Mosley's Fascist Party.

Immediately things got better for him and he was promoted from the sewage farm at Dortmumd to a sewage farm in Berlin – due to air raids there was more of it there. He cooperated with the Nazis and as a mark of appreciation they gave him extra sewage to handle. Then came the terrible Allied bombing raid on the city. Along with the residents, like *Starlight Express* he ran and ran and ran, then wandered lonely as a cloud that floats aloft o'er dale and hills when all at once he came upon a host of golden British Military Police. 'Oi, yew in the karzi suit, where yew goin?' Gollops explained he had escaped from a German top-security camp by killing twenty guards, they accepted his story, but just in case they beat him up. At his debriefing he told the officer he had a full working knowledge of Nazi sewage disposal. It was too good to waste, he was rushed back to England to become sanitary orderly to a bomb disposal unit in Leatherhead.

Those romantic war years were gone but not forgotten: whenever he heard Lili Marlene, his mind went back to those cooling sprinklers in Germany. He liked the Nazis; if Hitler were alive today there wouldn't be all these niggers and wogs in Kilburn. Hitler would stop all those niggers jumping up and down at discos, he'd put Velcro on the ceiling.

Gollops' bedroom was a temple to Fascism: above his head were newspaper cut-outs of Hitler, Franco, Mussolini and Mrs Thatcher, other walls have Swastikas and Nazi daggers, by the bed a copy of *Mein Kampf* 20p at Oxfam, the price of fame. The trouble with England was the Jews the niggers the wogs and his landlady Mrs Kitchen, the Royal family were Jews, wasn't Prince Charles circumscribed by the Chief Rabbi? Prince Philip was a Bubble-and-Squeak, Mountbatten was a bloody German, the Queen had wog blood through Isabella of Spain, Robert Graves said so. Hitler wouldn't have allowed all this pot smoking, he'd only have allowed decent non-homosexual Woodbines.

Like Nazi Germany, Gollops had his wife trained. When he went down for breakfast of a morning she'd give the Nazi salute and say, 'Mornin' darlin' and Heil 'Itler,' and he'd say, 'Mornin' darlin', Heil Hitler, what's fer breakfast,' and she'd

41

say, 'Weetabix and Heil Hitler.' Oh yes, Hitler was dead in the rest of the world but here at Flat 9, 345 Ivy Street, Kilburn, Hitler was alive and well. Gollops would never book a Mercedes or a Volkswagen. Today was a bad day for the Nordic race, Cooney the white boxing hope had been beaten by the nigger Larry Holmes. That nigger would never have knocked out Hitler, his Waffen SS would have crippled him in the first round with a Tiger Tank, oh yes.

This morning he came downstairs smelling of Brut and Sheen. 'Ohh, Heil 'Itler, darlin', you do look smart,' said Frau Gollops. Yes, today was Hitler's birthday, if Adolph were alive today he would have been dead forty years, today he would teach a few niggers a lesson.

This morning Len Gollops, traffic warden, walked the streets of Kilburn, his medals on, his shoes polished like Nazi jackboots, his hat steamed into the shape of the Waffen SS.

Ah! His heart leapt with joy, a rusting Mini Minor on a double yellow, velvet steering-wheel cover, skeleton doll hanging from rear-view mirror, Alsatian with nodding head in rear window, nylon imitation leopardskin upholstery, niggers!!! What's this note under the windscreen: 'The driver of this car is a crippled war hero, Dunkirk a direct hit.' Gollops' Fascist heart softened. As he put his tickets away, a tubby unshaven man arrived.

'Oh, officer,' he said. 'I'm just movin' it.'

'Are you Jewish?' said Gollops.

'No,' said the man. 'I can't afford to be.'

'Just a minute,' said Gollops. 'Did you write this note?' He held it before the man's eyes.

'I can't remember,' said the man, clutching his head. 'Loss of memory, the war, you know. Dunkirk, a direct hit!'

'It says here you're a war cripple.'

The man nodded.

'You walked all right to me, mate,' said Gollops.

The man suddenly grabbed his knee. 'Oh my legs.'

Staring at the unshaven man now rolling on the pavement, Gollops started to make out a ticket. 'I've 'ad enough of this bollocks,' he said.

The man groaned. 'Come here,' he said and crawling led Gollops round the back. 'Dere,' he said and pointed to a cardboard CD plate tied on with string. 'Irish Embassy,' said the man. 'You can't touch me,' he added and collapsed.

THE COURT CASE

A bureaucrat is a man who obeys orders from above and ignores complaints from below. So, to Clerk of Court Ruben Scratcher. His father Dick had been the last official hangman in Britain. Dick Scratcher, persecuted at school and at work for his name, sought his revenge by accepting the appointment as official hangman. For years he had a swinging time, then! the government had abolished capital punishment, consigning Dick Scratcher to the unemployment exchange at Catford, it was a human tragedy. Oh he tried, how he tried to get work: he tried the Gas Board, the Water Board, Battersea Dogs Home, Paul Raymond's Revue Bar, the Palladium, Harrods, none of them wanted a hangman. Came the day when in desperation he tried to hang himself, he bungled the job, he twisted his neck but was still alive. His wife was so ashamed that she was all for leaving him there. His son took pity and cut him down, fracturing his father's ankles, oh the disgrace! Bungling his own hanging! It was all too much, he died a broken man, a very broken one – a tram ran over him.

He had trained his son Ruben to inherit the job, young Ruben had looked forward to this. The hours as a boy he had spent making his own little gallows and hanging his sister's dolls, all that training wasted – the nearest to it was to work for the courts in the hope that one day the government would see sense and reintroduce the ancient craft of the hangman. Just in case, Ruben had kept all his father's old ropes in the attic. Once a week without fail, and sometimes with it, he oiled and waxed the ropes to keep them supple. On a beam he had a practice rope affixed to a weighted Neil Kinnock lookalike dummy that would drop through a trapdoor into the living-room below. A sympathiser had once asked him had he ever hung anybody. He had replied in the negative. 'Never mind,' said his friend. 'Where there's life there's hope.'

Now he sat in the well of the session court, he was neither criminal nor judge, he could neither sentence nor be sentenced, a perfect vacuum of safety. The first case today had been the accidental death of a Kilburn Irish gardener. A mosquito had flown into his earhole, try as he might he had tried to get it out, finally he shot it. The verdict: death by misadventure for the mosquito, accidental death for the Mick.

Next in the dock was a member of the Orange Sect, Sun of Brightness, will Sun of Brightness swear on the Bible? No, no, the Orange Sect disciple with his bald head, brown rice and orange wrapping will not, but he will swear on the *Lesbian Rastafarian Vegetarian Cookery Book*. What was the charge? Shoplifting a tin of fishpaste. Has Sun of Brightness anything to say? Yes, he is innocent! How did the tin arrive in his shopping bag? The tin, influenced by his charismatic magnetic karma, had levitated itself and landed of its own free will in his bag. Why hadn't he returned it to the shelf? Because the fishpaste wished to leave the corrupt environment of the supermarket and stay with him, its Om had willed it so. Had Sun of Brightness eaten the fishpaste? No, he had offered it to the world of nature. How? He gave it to the cat, it was the will of the cosmic force. 'It is the will of this court that Sun of Brightness, real name Percy Smith, pay a fine of fifty pounds or three moths in prison, which was better than three months in Scunthorpe.'

Chanting Hare Krishna Sun of Brightness was taken below where he quieted his disturbed Karma with a fag.

The magistrates recessed for lunch. These paragons of the legal Establishment meted out judgement on their, as feminists would have it, 'fellow persons'. None of them had ever set out in life to become magistrates, oh no, these appointments were circumstantial, usually from social contacts, say a soirée. 'He's a decent chap, let's put his name up' – it was as bent and as simple as that. It was to these that Mick Thomas Looney would plead his case.

45

There was Percival Cronk, sixty-nine, totally bald but he wore one of those wigs that can withstand the suction of a 747 jet engine – despite the guarantee, he was still paranoid about it being blown off. That awful evening on holiday in the Swiss Alps courting the rich American widow Anne Faulkner, that freak gust of wind had taken his wig up to the height of seven thousand feet depositing it on the Matterhorn, by then, too late! Mrs Faulkner knew his secret and left. He didn't know hers, a wooden leg. Traumatised, he rose every morning at five-thirty to hear any forecast of high winds – his wig could resist up to Gale Force Three, after that it was UHU or confined to home. He wasn't *that* fond of being a magistrate, but he liked the money and sometimes the women in the dock would have big tits. His housekeeper had big tits, and he constantly added to his collection of outsized brassières. When his housekeeper found them he explained, 'I keep them in memory of my dear wife's bosom.' When he died, they found the attic full of them on tailor's dummies, plus a photograph of him wearing one.

Then there was Priscilla Dobson, fifty-three, and a series of thirty-eights, divorced by a husband who could no longer tolerate her 'Mummie's little darlings', seven yapping Pekinese; people who didn't like yapping dogs weren't normal, *she* was normal. She, her seven yapping dogs, her Turganieff Green Goddess repro was normal! Her gardener going round the garden picking up dog turds with a pair of fire tongs was normal, her Doris Day, Charlie Kunz and Cha-Cha records were normal, her five hundred Mills and Boon paperbacks were normal, her 'Ladies' Friend' Yasimoto electric stimulator wasn't normal, but who was perfect?

The third member of the trio, Percy Pallot, sixty-eight, tall, thin, his black suit hanging on him like a shroud, a gaunt white face, although a red nose brought a touch of colour, was the most normal of the three. He just liked simple things: sausages, TV wrestling and little boys.

Free-lunched, the trio trooped back. 'The court will rise,' Looney in the dock hears the charges. 'Illegal use of CD plates, masquerading as a member of the Irish Embassy, no

46

driving licence, no insurance, no MOT test, no lights, no brakes, foul language, threatening violence, trying to bribe a traffic warden, also masquerading as a crippled war hero and finally trying, by guile, to extort money from a policeman.' Looney reeled, the clerk informed the court the accused has no solicitor.

'Is he capable of defending himself?'

'Oh yes, step outside and I'll show youse,' said Looney. The court broke into laughter.

'Order in court,' rapped Mr Cronk and brought his gavel down on his fountain pen, smashing it.

The court listened as the Pretender to the Irish throne rambled on about royal blood, his war service, Dunkirk a direct hit, a devout Roman Catholic, his long struggle with ill health, nursing a crippled wife and diseased mother and an invalid son with AIDS, supporting his relatives in Ireland and the London Irish Rugby Club, thus being of royal Irish blood, therefore demanding diplomatic immunity. 'Like dem bloody Arabs.'

A year's driving ban and fined twenty-five pounds, twenty-five pounds!!! That was nearly a thousand Guinnesses!

'You have seven days to pay,' said the clerk. 'The court can make it more.'

'Oh no,' said Looney, 'twenty-five pounds is enough.' He asked for time to pay, eighty years.

THE BUILDING SITE

The needle-sharp chill rain fell in cascades, the same rain that gave Britain the world's lead in arthritis, making the British possibly the most miserable race on earth, where the national sport appeared to be coughing it up.

However, this gloom was broken by the cheerful sound of Looney's cement-mixer. Despite his new throne, despite his cardboard CD plates, despite his royal blood, he was still mixing cement for Mowlems, the English suppressor of free Ireland. No one believed his regal claims, only one very perceptive labourer, Tim Foggerty the site tea boy, he believed in Looney's claims. He also believed that Prince Philip came from Outer Space, if you ate enough boiled eggs you could live without breathing and Chinamen were decended from bananas.

'Listen, Foggerty,' said Looney, placing a hand on his shoulder for a rest, 'how much money has youse got on youse?' Looney spoke very slowly — Foggerty had a Titanic mind, more than four consecutive words were like an iceberg to him.

How much money? Foggerty thought. After five minutes he said, 'Three pounds,' or was it after three minutes five pounds, never mind, either would do.

'How would you like to be me Chancellor of the Exchequer?' Yes, he'd like that fine. The Pretender continued, 'Now dis appointment, I want youse ter keep it a secret, I don't want every Tom, Dick or Harry ter know.' Foggerty made a mental note never to tell anybody called Tom, Dick or Harry.

'Youse understand, Foggerty?' After three attempts the lad nodded his head. 'Good, now yer job his to put a pound on dis horse.' He handed the lad a slip of paper.

'Dis isn't a horse,' he said, 'it's a bit of paper.' Regal life was frustrating. 'No lad, dat is a royal bettin' slip, now off youse goes.'

Foggerty wasn't that thick. 'Ain't you puttin' any money on?'

Looney gave a kingly wave. 'People of royal blood never handle money, youse don't see the Queen givin' Prince Philip 50p ter put on horses.'

'No,' said Foggerty. 'Dat's because he's from Outer Space and you can't trust dem.'

'Don't argue,' said Looney, 'or I'll deport youse.'

Off went Foggerty, Looney watching the clumping lumbering lad as he was gradually swallowed up in the drenching rain. Looney was well pleased. Now the bad news, the rain stopped.

'Orl rite,' said the Cockney foreman. 'Orl you tea-drinkin' bastards back ter work.'

The Pretender returned to his cement-mixer.

king looney of clare in purple lurex evening dress and silver lamé wellington boots picked up his jewel-encrusted tea mug and drained the last of the champagne. the royal site foreman came to the georgian hut door. the king floored him with a punch.

'get up, yer cockney bastard,' he said. 'lick der mud off dem boots.'

'yes, your majesty,' said the royal foreman. 'i've just come, your majesty, to tell you that it's stopped rainin' so you can get back to work again.'

king looney floored him with a punch. 'get up, you cockney bastard ii.' he then threw a few million more pound notes on the fire to keep it going.

ah, here comes lord foggerty, financial wizard and the royal chancellor of the exchequer. 'good news, your majesty,' he said, and emptied a massive sack of money on the floor.

'der horse won,' king looney smiled.

'it was a good idea you stopping all the other horses running,' said the chancellor.

'here,' said king looney, 'here's your pound back.' he looked at the half-built drool castle, better get on.

king looney floored the foreman. 'get up, you cockney bastard iii, and carry me,' he ordered. the royal foreman put on a pair of white gloves and lifted the king on to his head. 'put me down by der royal cement-mixer.' followed by the workmen singing 'danny boy'. the foreman lowered him to the ground. with another punch he floored the foreman. 'get up, you cockney bastard iv.'

the king started to shovel cement mixed with diamonds into his solid gold cement-mixer. he had pride, one day his descendants would mix cement...

Wot luck, it was raining again. Back in the workmen's hut Looney warmed his hands by the brazier, what is this figure like a lake on legs looming in the distance? From it emerged the Chancellor of the Exchequer, water dripping from his every garment, squelching in his boots. Hyper-ventilating, he collapsed in a soggy steaming heap of his monarch's feet. Bad news! Looney's horse fell at the first fence, Looney lost his bet, Foggerty lost his job. Never mind, something else would come along, pneumonia.

THE THRINS

Mr and Mrs Hercules Thrin were fifty now, not likely to have any more children. Eh? Ha ha, no, thought Hercules as he mustard-seeded the windowbox for the summer, the last time they'd done it, yes, it was the time they went to the Wasdale Road Astoria, Forest Hill to see Edmund O'Brien in *Dead on Arrival*. Yes, that was the last time, or was it? No! It *wasn't Dead on Arrival*, it was another film, it was *High Noon* with Gary Cooper, they saw that, they saw *High Noon* and when they got back they didn't do it, *that* was the last time, because, it was so cold they decided *not* to do it. They had a glass of Emu sherry instead, that's it. Sharon had gone to the lounge sideboard and said, 'Look, Hercules, this Emu sherry's been here a long time, we'd better finish it up.' Yes, no wait! They *did* do it that night, yes, that's it, and it *wasn't* Emu sherry, it was Cyprus sherry – what was the brand name? Andromeda! *That* was it, Andromeda sherry! Sharon had said, 'We might as well finish the bottle.' Yes, that was the name of the sherry the last time they did it, it was very reasonable, six shillings a bottle, yes, six shillings a bottle, that was the last time they did it. It must have been Andromeda because whenever he was in Tesco's and saw a bottle of Andromeda sherry he was reminded that it was the last time they did it, no wait! Ah! He had got it wrong, it *was* Andromeda sherry but the film wasn't *High Noon* with Gary Cooper, no, it was John Mills in *Ice Cold in Alex*, better just check that with Sharon. Good God he was wrong all the time, Sharon remembers the last time – it was New Year's Eve 1969 when they went to see Frank Sinatra in *The Man with the Golden Arm*, they came back and Sharon went to the lounge sideboard and brought out a bottle of Emu sherry, so after all that it *wasn't* the Andromeda sherry but the *Emu*. That was the last time they'd done it, what a silly he had been, all these years going to Tesco's and each time he'd seen Andromeda sherry he'd thought, Ah! that reminds me of the last time we did it, what a fool and a waste of time. It went to show how easily you could mistake one sherry for another, especially as one came from Cyprus and the other from Australia. Well, that was settled, he was glad he had got it right in the end – *The Man with the Golden Arm* with John Mills and *Emu* sherry. So yes, no more children, he could sell the old bassinet it was still in good condition, he oiled it regularly, a few extra quid could buy a bottle of Emu sherry. Put an ad in the papers, abbreviation saves money; Fr. Sale. Bass, £3 o.n.o.

Dick Looney couldn't believe his eyes, he looked up from his plate of Crispies Ricicles that had been fired from cannons, refortified with spray-on vitamins, artificial colouring E 386409567, inverted milk, emulsifiers, and artificial flavouring E94785638965, and read the small ads. A bass for £3.00 o.n.o.? How he yearned to be seen playing that £3 o.n.o. bass! He wanted to be up there in the flashing strobe lights with dry-ice clouds seeping up the legs of his glitter leather trousers, his pink and green mohican hairdo tossing in the laser beams, singing out in a million megawatt sound system, 'Ah lurves ya baby – I loves ya – baby I lurves ya yes I do, I do, I do do do.'

Hercules Thrin clenched the cheeks of his bum and answered the door. Standing there in a huge concertina suit was a spotty lad held together with acne, hair oil and St Michael's underwear. The sun shone through his protruding ears silhouetting the veins like the canals on Mars, a little coconut sprout of hair projected from the top of his head, the lad gave a grin the shape and size of an Egyptian sunboat.

'I've come in answer to the £3 o.n.o.,' he said. Was it still for sale? Yes it was.

'Yours is the thirteenth £3 o.n.o. we've had this morning,' lied Thrin. 'It's in the garden shed,' he added.

Dick followed Thrin through the house. 'Excuse the mess,

only we've got the Conservatives in,' he joked. Thrin liked a joke, Dick didn't like it.

In the garden a small cock sparrow called Nigel landed on the garden shed a-chirruping a-plenty. Unbeknown to Dick or Thrin he had just had a fly called Tom for breakfast. Not many flies are called Tom for breakfast.

'You're a bit young to be having children,' said Mr Thrin. 'When's the baby due?'

Dick told him he wasn't having a baby and that's why it wasn't due.

'Oh,' said Mr Thrin. 'Somebody else having a baby?'

No, nobody else is having a baby.

'Then what do you want it for?'

'I want to learn to play it,' said Dick.

'Play it?' said Mr Thrin, unclenching the cheeks of his bum. 'You must be joking.'

'Oh no,' said Dick. 'I'm not joking.'

Thrin clenched unclenched and reclenched the cheeks of his bum. 'How can you *play* one with a baby in it?'

What was this man talking about? thought Dick, and about Dick, Thrin thought, What is this boy talking about?

On the roof Nigel the sparrow ate Morris the caterpillar.

'I'm not going to have a baby in it,' said Dick. 'I want to play it in a band.'

Now Mr Thrin was worried, this boy could be on drugs.

'The Beatles have one, and they don't have a baby in theirs,' went on the drugged lad.

'Well,' said Mr Thrin, 'I better warn you that this has already had a baby in it.' Mr Thrin entered the shed and reappeared with the bassinet, whipping off the dustcover. 'Voilà,' he said.

This didn't fool young Dick. 'That isn't a voilà, that's a pram.' Mr Thrin knew it was a pram. 'Where is the £3 Bass o.n.o.?' said disappointed Dick.

The two men paused and stared at each other for identically different reasons. On the shed above Nigel the sparrow paused, making it three identically different pauses, except the sparrow's which was higher up. Mr Thrin and his unclenched

53

bum were getting impatient. 'This *is* the Bassinet, £3 o.n.o.,' he said, showing Dick the wording on the advert. All became clear. Chirrup-chirrup, went the sparrow, real happiness was a fly called Tom for breakfast and a caterpillar called Morris.

THE ILLNESS

A NHS doctor's waiting-room, it had the same electric ambience as cattle waiting at the knacker's yard. Today owners of bronchitis, piles, arthritis, scrofula, boils, mange, were slumped in chairs around the walls, all silent and still like Roman funerary statues – only not as cheerful. Looney and his son Dick entered and were greeted with those suggestive stares that range from a court martial to interfering-with-little-girls. He sat himself down next to a mountain of a woman with a plastic bag on her South Col, and a small boy whose nose streamed like a Niagara and seemed to be visibly shrinking in size. They all sat in a silence that one could only find on Mars. The bronchitis was in charge of Les Warner, a Securicor guard, an expert in unarmed combat, judo, karate; despite all this vigilance, a bronchitis had got in. The piles owner was Mortimer Slench, an accountant. He could outspeed an abacus in counting, he could even outcount a computer and an electric adding machine, but he had never counted on getting piles.

The arthritis was the outright property of Lavinia Kerenski. She was a teacher of Russian dancing. Her pupils wondered why she spent so much time in the squatting position, it was simple: once down, she couldn't get up again, she used to bid her puzzled pupils assume the squatting position, then she would let out a scream while her husband stretched her into the upright position. She only believed in homoeopathic medicine: at first she tied carrots to the backs of her knees and dripped candle wax on to her patellas; that failed. She tried Mrs Patrick Furg who placed sunflower seeds under her tongue and enemas of oil of violets up the rectum; it didn't

55

work. Next the dear woman made her drink nettle tea and rubbed her buttocks with olive oil and French mustard; it didn't work. Then there were the freezing cold baths and ice packs in the groins; this worked, it gave her pneumonia. Now she sat in the squatting position in the corner of the waiting-room reading Tolstoy.

It was Guardsman Leech who had the Scorfulus, (the reader can look this up himself – it's something like 'Inflammation of the Guardsman').

The mountainous woman, without turning her head, spoke to Looney, '' 'Ees slow terday.'

Looney grasped the challenge; she was imparting know-ledge that suggested that someone who was normally fast, was now slow today. Who could that be? He'd try an answer. 'Does he drive a car?' he said, looking ahead.

She replied, 'Suppose so, ah suppose so.'

He was getting warmer. 'Is he in the room?' said Looney, who loved a challenge.

'Eh?' said she, looking ahead.

'Is he in the room?' said Looney

'No . . . 'ee's in the next room, isn't 'ee?'

Got it! thought Looney. 'It's the doctor,' he triumphed.

As he spoke, a black Jamaican nurse with a water-melon smile issued from the surgery. 'Meesers Pronk?' she said. From the corner arose a dear old lady, her address must have been Highgate Cemetery. She gave a toothless grin of acknowledgement, she rose as though it was Judgement Day, as slowly as the growth of a geranium seed in spring, clasping a walking stick that was more alive than her, she tottered across the room, all eyes following her doddering progress like the last episode of *Dynasty*. She'll be lucky if she comes back, thought Looney. She was followed by the boils and the mange. Finally, four hours older and impregnated with waiting-room germs, it was the Looneys' turn.

Looney and his son Dick were in the presence of Dr Ralph Fees. Carefully he took down their personal details. 'Now,' he said, 'what can *I* do for you?' Every time he spoke his eyebrows, which looked like two hairy giant caterpillars above his eyes, shot up and down.

'Well, sir,' said Looney, 'fer tirty years now I been payin' into der National Health Service.' The eyebrows semaphored understanding. 'In all dat time none of me family have ever had an illness.'

'Oh, you're very lucky,' said Fees.

'Lucky?' queried Looney. 'I don't tink so, sir, I must have paid in tousands of pounds into der NHS and I never had any value fer me money, nuttin', not even a common cold.'

The eyebrows waggled in irritation. 'Look, Mr Looney, I'm a doctor not an accountant, I'm a very busy man I have lots of patients.'

Looney pulled his chair closer. 'If youse got lots of patience, wot's der hurry?'

Fees removed his glasses, turning the two Looneys into a blur, a distinct improvement.

Looney pulled his chair a little closer. 'We want you to give us an illness.'

Down came the eyebrows halfway and stayed there. 'My good fellow, I can't do that.'

Looney pulled his chair a little closer. 'Why not? It would be good for business.'

Fees replaced his glasses which showed that Looney was now two feet nearer and coming down the side of his desk. 'Mr Looney, I have taken the Hippocratic Oath.'

Looney chuckled, 'Don't worry, doc, I swear meself.' He pulled his chair nearer, he was now almost by the doctor's side. 'How much is a good illness, nuttin' serious like AIDS, say a bronchitis?'

The eyebrows converged over the bridge of the nose, they looked at the ceiling. Why oh why wasn't euthanasia official? 'Well, bronchitis,' said the doctor, moving his chair back a bit, 'say antibiotics, nostrums, aspirins, Vick Vapour Rub, say three visits, that should be about four hundred pounds.'

'Dat's lovely,' said Looney. 'Four hundred pounds, now what's der best way ter get dat illness? Mind you, I don't want it, oh no, I have to go to work, no, me son's out of work so he can have it.'

Looney drew his chair closer, Fees pulled his back a bit, gradually the two men were leaving the room. 'All right, Mr Looney, if you sit your son in my waiting-room every day he's bound to catch something, now please . . .'

THE VOYAGE

Looney had vague memories of Drool village from when he was a boy, but then, only having left it four hours ago, he only had vague memories of Kilburn as a man. Now here he was, or rather there he was in Holyhead boarding the night ferry to Dún Laoghaire. A sturdy little vessel, *The Song of Erin*, it disturbed the crew that the Captain always slept in the lifeboat.

It was midnight as the little steam packet left the harbour – the last time Looney had caught a packet was in Cairo. It was a perfect English summer's night as the steamer left the harbour into the teeth of a Force Nine gale; great drenching waves full of fishes and nuclear waste swept over the ship's prow.

'A fine bloody time ter book us as deck passengers,' said Mrs Looney.

'I was tryin' ter save money,' said himself.

'If dis gets worse we'll be tryin' ter save our bloody lives,' she said, the nuclear-discharge salt spray dripping from her face.

'Well, it's safer dan flying,' he said.

'Flying isn't dangerous,' she said, '*crashing* is dangerous.'

By Looney's side sat Prince. He had promised to give the farting dog as a present along with the parrot to his brother, it would be a relief to get rid of them. To keep the dog warm they dressed him in an old sports jacket and there it sat with its front legs through the sleeves – to the shortsighted it would appear to be a midget in the kneeling load position. Inside Looney's jacket pocket the talkative parrot was peacefully sleeping off the Mickey Finn. An oil-skinned, glistening seaman slithered and slid towards-and-away-towards-and-

59

away-and-towards-and-sideways-towards-them-backwards-round-and-forward-towards-them again.

'He's never goin' ter get here,' said Looney.

From where he was, the oil-skinned sailor grabbed the railings and shouted, 'Ahoy, me hearties! The Captain said it's too dangerous out 'ere, you got ter go round the back, follow me.' He turned and slithered in the direction of away-sideways-up-and-down-round-then-away-again. He led them aft to the ship's laundry and drying room, at one end of which hung tablecloths, sheets, pillowcases and a mass of crew's garments.

'God, dey must all be naked up there,' said Looney.

The journey was spent with Mrs Looney and her son taking it in turns to be sick. Looney himself wasn't sick, but he was sick of them being sick, and they were sick of him being sick of them. A gay sailor entered and minced towards some underwear. 'Ooooo!' he said. 'Wot you all doin' in the airing cupboard?' Looney stiffened, a queer! AIDS! he thought and held his breath until the seaman departed. If he was King of Ireland he wouldn't have poofs in his navy . . .

hms de valera, the irish navy's latest battleship, stood ready for the launch. the ten-foot-long leather battleship stood at an alarming angle on the ramps, its side still glistening with pitch and wet tar. flies, gnats and insects by the thousand were getting stuck to it. six hello-sailors stood at their oars. the launching platform was crammed with shamrock-green dignitaries. queen looney the first was there and wearing a fine c&a mode frock embroidered with harps, and der glitter stockings 'like dat singer lyndsey the paul'. she was holding a litre bottle of eec poteen 90% proof on the end of a piece of string tied to the neck of court jester ian paisley, who leapt up and down shouting 'no popery here', only to be floored by club-wielding courtiers when they jumped on his head to musical accompaniment.

admiral king looney stood in the prow of the ship throwing pound notes and autographed contraceptives to the dockyard workers. he himself was wearing the expensive flannel trousers, der pockets full of gold and luncheon vouchers and a cowboy hat like dat jr wears when he's not screwing mandy. then everyone started doing a ceilidh. they ceilidhed all over the floor. then there was a distribution of baked spuds which royal potato-throwers hurled into the crowds. then the bagpipes played glen miller's 'in the mood' and they all ate der potatoes in time to der music.

then the queen raised the bottle of poteen, shouting, 'I name dis boat der hms de valera, god help all who sail on her.' she hurled the bottle at the ship, followed by ian paisley. the poteen hit king looney straight between the eyes. with the sailors rowing furiously, the boat, slid majestically to the water and sank to the bottom to join the rest of the irish navy.

The dawn came up like thunder out of China, 'cross the bay, in Dún Laoghaire it didn't come up at all.

Tim McGuggles, the dawn customs officer, waited vengefully for the next batch of passengers. Last night's affair was still fresh in his yellow chalk mind. Eileen Holes, the girl *he* had taken body-building lessons for, had *his* teeth straightened for, had a hair transplant for, had *his* teeth capped for, had *his* varicose veins operated on for, had a vasectomy for, wore black and red striped underwear for, bought a waterbed for, had gone off with Ruth le Mottles, the black Rastafarian lesbian! Just when *he* wanted to. Someone would pay for this! It appeared to be him. He started with this first batch of shivering passengers.

'That dog,' he snapped. 'Quarantine!' He snatched the string from Looney's hand and tied the dog to the bench. 'Open your bags,' he snarled; that lovely black body going out with another *woman*!

'Wese got nuttin' to declare,' said Looney.

'They all say that,' said McGuggles. 'You could be carrying illegal currency.'

'Jasus, we'd be grateful if you find any,' said salt-sea-soaked Mrs Looney.

Inside Looney's pocket the parrot had revived, refreshed by his long sleep. 'Tweak yer willy, sailor,' it squawked.

'What did you say?' said McGuggles.

'Nuttin',' said Looney.

'I didn't hear you say nuttin',' said McGuggles as he stirred the contents of the Looneys' luggage into a great cloth porridge, he'd teach that black lesbian cow.

'Tweak yer willy, sailor.'

McGuggles frowned. 'What did you say?'

61

'I didn't say nuttin',' insisted Looney

'I thought you did, I thought I heard you say tweak yer willy, sailor.'

'I said no such ting.'

'Tweak yer willy, sailor.'

'There! You said it again!' insisted McGuggles, and why was this passenger suddenly hitting himself violently in the chest?

''Tis the indigestion,' thumped Looney.

A big crowd was building up, he'd show 'em all not to let a black Rastafarian lesbian and bad typist give him the elbow. I mean, what good is an elbow in bed?

'Here,' he said, 'here's a receipt for the dog.'

'Don't give it to him,' said Looney. 'He can't read.'

'Move on,' roared McGuggles.

Behind the enraged customs man the dog let off several quick canine ones. McGuggles sniffed, My God what was that? Where was it coming from? Silently Prince filled the area, passengers' eyes started to water, all looked suspiciously at McGuggles, customs officers tried opening windows and doors. The Looneys heard racing footsteps approaching: McGuggles, a handkerchief over his nose, handed the animal back to them. 'Take the bloody thing,' he gasped.

THE MEETING

Brother Shamus had promised to meet them and provide transport. The Looneys stood under the dockyard clock, eight o'clock! And waiting, waiting; a gusting wind blew an empty ice-cream carton across the street, its fructose contents now in the stomach of Rose McCafferty aged six, holding her mother's hand and still dreaming of a yesterday ice-cream. She had eaten it very slowly, the green part first then the chocolate and then the vanilla. She had kept each spoonful in her mouth until the last drop had melted, she didn't often get ice-cream, you don't when your da's in the Maze prison and yer mommy goes out scrubbing.

Eight o'clock and still no sign of his brother. 'What time did he says he was comin'?' said Mrs Looney.

Himself turned his head, raindrops like pearls circumnavigated the brim of his trilby. 'He didn't say,' he said.

'Did *you* say what time?' says she.

'No,' says he. 'I didn't say any time so neider of us would be late.'

Still eight o'clock, it was eight o'clock for a long time in Ireland.

'How in God's name does he keep an appointment?' she insisted.

'He goes by the sun,' he said.

'There is no bloody sun.'

'Ah, dat's why he's late.'

Still eight o'clock! Looney had a quick tally of his financial holdings, he was a suspicious man – to get money out of him his wife used a metal detector. See now, he had twenty pounds distributed around his body, ten pounds sewn in a moneybelt around his waist, three pounds in coins in various pockets,

63

another three pounds sewn in his sock, two pounds affixed with Elastoplast in his jockstrap and finally several pound coins sewn in his hatband. He reasoned that if he were mugged the criminal would die of exhaustion looking for it.

Eight o'clock! Whippets of rain slashed the air, the streets looked varnished with glycerine, the parrot was recovering consciousness for the second time. Soon Looney was explaining to the crowd how he could say 'Tweak your willy, sailor' without moving his lips and by merely hitting his chest.

'For God's sake,' said herself. 'Hit him any more and he'll be a bloody bookmarker.'

Still eight o'clock! Surely things can't be this bad in Ireland, here at twenty past eleven, dead on eight o'clock by the dockyard clock, comes Shamus with a horse and dung cart!

'Top of der mornin' to youse,' said Shamus, the image of his twin brother, but worse, identically worse.

Soggily the Looneys boarded the dung cart, they drove away before a bemused crowd to the sound of 'Tweak yer willy, sailor' and a man thumping his chest trying to drown out the animal shouting 'Nilgiri Hills tea-growing area in western India'.

THE SHOE SALE

Across the Irish Sea, away from all this, in comfortable Wimbledon but a stone's throw from Caesar's Camp, Colonel Ronald Jenkins, ex-Indian Army Pay Corps, stood in the bay window of his semi-detached second-mortgaged house. He looked at his duty-free watch, time for a duty-free gin and tonic, Molly his duty-free wraith-like wife thumbed through a dentist's waiting-room copy of *Country Life* 1933.

Jenkins, red, rotund, bellicose, lit his duty-free cigar, shook a plus-foured leg to alleviate certain dermal adhesions in his groins, and returned his duty-free lighter to his Oxfam waistcoat pocket; it was good to have a son who was an air steward. What wasn't so good was him about to become a stewardess. However, he/she still got the duty-frees. Colonel Jenkins shook the other leg and gained considerable relief. Pity about the Dunlop shares, another sip of the duty-free. Ah! Those golden India days when he was a pukka sahib.

Suddenly Jenkins froze, it was nothing to do with the heating, no. 'My God, Molly,' he gasped. 'There's a wog coming up the garden path!'

'Where?' said Molly, half rising.

'No, don't look, dear, if they see a white woman they go berserk!'

It was an old Indian from Amsterdam in a shabby World War Two demob suit and trilby. God! Jenkins knew they'd got as far as Southall, but *Wimbledon*! This was the thin end. He watched the wog as he reached the door. Outside, Bapu Lalkaka put his Tesco's Union Jack shopping bag down on the step and rang the bell. That long journey from Calcutta had nearly destroyed his shoes. Luckily he had spotted the advert: 'For Sale, stout walking shoes, property of an English

65

gentleman, must sell, owner going bankrupt. £6 o.n.o.'. He pressed the doorbell. From inside Jenkins cocked a shotgun and peered through the letterbox.

'Clear out, you Hindu swine! We had relatives in the black hole of Calcutta!'

Lalkaka was stunned. 'I'm not from Calcutta,' he said, 'hi am from Kilburn.'

The voice replied, 'We had relatives in that black hole as well!'

Jenkins waited no more. Thrusting the muzzle through the letterbox, he fired, it blasted Lalkaka's shopping bag to shreds, rice and curry powder littered the front garden.

'You swine, you've curried me geraniums,' shouted the Colonel.

'No no, please please,' said Lalkaka. 'I have come to buy the walking shoes.'

So now wogs were wearing shoes! From inside the house there was a pregnant silence, it gave birth to Jenkins' eyes at the letterbox. 'The shoes?' he said.

'Yes, the shoes,' said Lalkaka.

Lalkaka heard the door chain go on. Slowly it peaked open and the face of Jenkins appeared in the slit.

'You have money?' he said.

Lalkaka nodded.

'With the Queen's head on?'

Again Lalkaka nodded.

'Wait here,' said Jenkins. 'I'll go and get them.'

He retreated behind the door, and one Colonel later the door slowly opened to reveal Jenkins, now barefooted, holding a pair of shoes. 'There,' he said. 'I've, er, I've been keeping them warm for you.'

Taking the proffered shoes, Lalkaka sat on the step and took his off. 'I am seeing if they are fitting.'

Jenkins glared. 'Of *course* they're fit, I wouldn't wear them otherwise!'

Lalkaka stood, stamped the new shoes on the ground crushing an ant called Norris. He then set off up the garden and up the road.

'I say! What are you doing?' said Jenkins, following at a trot.

'I am road-testing them,' said Lalkaka.

'They've *been* road-tested, I tell you! I've done over eight hundred miles in them, I've still got a Harrods receipt with the date on.'

Lalkaka stopped and smiled, he counted out six pounds into the Colonel's trembling hand.

'Has he gone?' asked the wraith-like Molly.

'I drove him off, dear,' said Jenkins, taking up his unfinished gin and tonic. His eyes narrowed, wogs in Wimbledon! To think his grandfather used to tie 'em to the mouths of cannons and blow them away. He looked at his duty-free watch, time for another duty-free . . .

THE ACCIDENT

The horse-drawn entourage reached the outskirts of what was once beautiful Georgian Dublin, now ravaged by the idiot city fathers who sired bastard buildings. The grey galleon clouds departed like fleeing Danes, and like a victorious Brian Boru the sun shone. The sun! People pointed at the flaming orb, some knelt and crossed themselves, others reported it to the Gardai, many took photographs, some even confessed it to the priest who came out and blessed it proclaiming a miracle. Donagh McDonagh the fiery patriotic poet declaimed:

> Ohhhhh fiery Celtic sun,
> Come fill us with your holy Catholic light.
> You rarely come by day
> And practically never at night.

It wasn't the Looneys' idea of a holiday, huddled together in the back of a dung cart.
'Would youse like something ter eat?' shouted Shamus.
'Oh yes,' replied Looney.
'God, so would I,' replied Shamus, and that was that.
While Shamus had his head averted it happened.
'Dere's been a crash up dere, a hoss has run into a funeral,' said Milly McGroins, who couldn't wait to tell people about crashes. The Catholic horse had seen a Protestant and shied. Like Starsky and Hutch, Shamus slewed the cart to take evasive action but like the Dukes of Hazzard crashed into the hearse. A little wimp of a mortician, his top hat askew, frothed, 'I saw that! You might have killed somebody!' he said, inadvertently pointing to the coffin.

Inside, in its satin confines was the body of Alan O'Hanrahan. The Ballsbridge clairvoyant who had so frequently contacted the dead was now one himself. There was Mrs Rita Cake, the last living survivor of the Rudolph Valentino fan club. Just the week before, deep in a poteen-induced trance, O'Hanrahan had failed to raise the great matinee idol, however he had managed to contact Valentino's dog and his plumber. He had foretold the future of so many people it was a pity that he did not foretell that Mrs Higgs' husband would come into the bedroom while he was screwing her, and shoot him. As if that wasn't bad enough, here he was in an unpredicted accident.

'Now den, wot's dis all about?' said Garda Tombs, ducking under the prancing horse.

'Gis a hand ter get der coffin back in,' said a straining mortician's attendant.

'Who was he?' said Looney just to make conversation.

'He was a clairvoyant,' they said.

'Oh,' said Looney, pretending he knew what that meant. 'He must be a great loss to der company.'

'What about the dent in me hearse?' said the mortician, who now had his hat on straight but his head on sideways.

'Don't get excited,' said Tombs. 'Man, the funeral's due at St Brides in ten minutes, if we miss dat he'll have to go back in cold storage till the next vacancy.' Tombs set to taking details. He needed a good accident, it was better than tellin' hundreds of Japanese where Bernard Shaw lived or where the relief massage parlours were. This accident had romance, drama, a dung cart, a dead spiritualist and a horse! He recorded all the names including the stiff.

'Fer God's sake, hurry up,' said the desperate voice of the widow, 'or he'll start to go off.'

It was a grand accident for the Dubliners, lots of them brought out chairs and had their lunch at it, the mourners took it in turns to bring 'restorative cordials' from the pub. Sean Teeth, an inspector from the RSPCA had arrived and insisted the horse be fed and watered, culminating with him giving it a pizza and Guinness. American tourists were

69

impressed: 'Look, Wilbur, isn't it cute, a real Irish accident.' After posing for photos by Japanese tourists the accident broke up and went its way. To strangled squawks of 'Tweak yer willy, sailor', the Looneys drove on.

'God, I'm hungry,' said Looney.

'Wait till we get outside of Dublin,' said Shamus, 'der food's cheaper.'

'Dat's because it's worse,' said Mrs Looney.

THE VILLAGE OF DROOL

The village of Drool slumbered in its unending tissue of mist-haunted rain, lost in what seemed like a timeless valley encased in nodding green hills. It all rested on the bones of the giant Irish elk buried in tissues of basalt black peat underfoot, where lay million-year-old mutating Irish oaks. Fat, patched cattle mooed in lush shamrock-strewn meadows; cuddling the village like a liquid arm ran the River Murragh; sliding in its watery music, wary of fly-decked hooks, were the glittering homing salmon, the river princes.

Many a moon-mad night Rory Mullins and Father Dan Costello dipped their illegal nets and scooped up plump supper-promised trout while Garda O'Brien kept an eye out for the law. There had been that fatal star-kissed night, all three were caught by Sergeant Kelly. He had let them off with a caution and a bribe, confiscated the salmon and sold it to his superintendant.

As the Looney entourage passed through the main street, little pink pinched faces peered through little windows, eyes following them, lips made for gossip spoke, ' 'Tis shamus Looney with a smell s and dat rich brudder from the London.' The same Shamus Looney who had sired ten kids in ten years, whose poor wife had pleaded with Father Costello, 'Father we can't afford another child.'

The Pope-orientated priest spoke sternly: this woman wanted to take the accursed Protestant Pill. 'No, Mrs Looney, 'tis mortal sin to take that sinful terrible pill.'

'But I don't want any more kids,' she said.

'Then,' said the priest, 'you must *stop* the sexual intercourse!'

'Listen, father,' she said, 'I don't have intercourse with him, he has it with *me*, he does it while I'm asleep!'

71

'Don't you ever wake up?'

'God, no father, I'm too tired.'

'Then how do you know he does it.'

'Nine months later!'

Costello sent for Shamus. 'Listen, man, you must stop havin' the sexual intercourses with yer wife when she's asleep.'

'Oh, it seems a pity ter wake her up father, I do it as quiet as possible.'

'You *must* stop it, man! You must use the rhythm method.'

Shamus's brows ruffled. 'Rhythm method? Wot's dat?'

'It means you only do it at certain times.'

'I always do it at certain times, twenty past twelve.'

'Look, read this book, it's by the Pope, it explains all the method.'

How could *he* know about it? No one in the Vatican screwed! Shamus took time learning how to open the book, he read it and re-read it. Good God, here was the church telling people when and how to screw, intercourse was *only* meant to begat children! That's what the sex act was for, Tommy Cooper had a better act than that! While Shamus Looney's family slept four in a bed the Pope slept luxuriously alone.

Just outside Drool, Shamus reined up the horse. 'Dis is it,' he said, pointing to a blot on the landscape. 'Dis is der cottage. Four walls, a fireplace, a few sticks of furniture, no more. Still, it's free,' said Shamus.

'I should tink so,' said Mrs Looney. 'No one in dere right bloody mind would pay for dis.' She dumped down her rain-soaked bags on the floor.

'It'll look better when youse has yer bits and pieces in,' said Shamus.

'It's *all* bits and bloody pieces,' she said.

'I'll get der fire goin',' said Looney, breaking up a chair.

'Oh, we got der electric,' boasted Shamus, switching on the light.

'God, it looked better in the dark,' said Mrs Looney.

72

'Will youse stop complaining!' said Looney. 'Dis is only temporary.'

'Dat's fer sure,' she said. 'It won't last the bloody night.'

Above the door was a holy picture of the Sacred Heart – 'I will bless the house wherein this picture is shown' – something had gone wrong.

In the coming weeks, bit by bit, the cottage was put into shape, a coat of whitewash here, a shelf there, a bit of plasterwork, a wall here, a floor and a roof there. It was hard work but Mrs Looney finally finished it. Drool! This was where the seat of the family was and he was sitting on it! Searching for his royal ancestry Looney asked the folks around about his royal father and grandfather, sure they *all* knew them. 'Oh, those two cunts,' they'd say.

THE DAY OF HIMSELF

It was the day, March the Seventeenth, that Drool celebrated its favourite saint. The Saint and Scholar pub reeled under the alcoholic assault. Irishmen in steaming clutches lay stupefied in a series of grotesque positions, there were happy cross-eyed idiot smiles on their faces. From either end they expelled a mist of only-drunk-once whiskey fumes, one watch could have set off the first Celtic atom bomb. From inside the pub further groups of Irishmen were training to join the unconscious alcoholics outside on the pavement. At intervals, to drunken singing, fresh bodies were carried out and let go with a thud on the pavement. There was a time-honoured ritual of emptying the man's pockets. An old Drool saying goes, 'What good is money to the unconscious?' All stocks of the hard stuff had gone, they were drinking something being made in a bath that tasted like lighter fuel mixed with crushed woodlice.

It was well after midnight in the billiards room, the table was covered with the recently unconscious, in fact there were now more balls on the table than ever before. The crack was in full swing, important songs were being sung, slightly inter-woven. 'Ohhhhh,' sang a wavering drunk, 'a little bit of Danny boy fell from out of Mother Macree alive-aliveo One dayyyyyyyyy,' and fell back into the soft Celtic night on to the hard Celtic pavement. Looney and his brother sat in the corner, they only stopped drinking to top up from the dregs of others.

'Here,' said a bald, red-faced, reeking monster with a fiddle, 'I'll play youse a tune.'

'Do you play requests?' said Looney.

'What would you like?' said the man.

'Oh, anything,' said Looney.

He placed the instrument in between two unshaven double chins. 'What's it to be?' says he.

They'd like 'I'll Take You Home Again, Cathleen'. There started a wailing tinny sound. At first they concluded the man was tuning up, but then it went on too long for that. The hairy fiddler had his eyes closed, was it inspiration? No, it was a sneeze coming, 'AHTISHOO.' He was well into it but this wasn't the Cathleen they all knew, this Cathleen was bent double, totally bald, smoking a pipe, this was Cathleen pissed and up before the beak for shoplifting. With a flourish that threw him off balance, the fiddler fell back into the soft Celtic night, joining the rest.

Rory Mullins the publican was talking to Looney. 'So youse is a stranger round here,' he said.

'Yes, I'm a stranger round here.' He pointed to a corner. 'If I was there, I would be a stranger there as well but not in London, there I'm not a stranger as well.'

'The London, is it?'

'Yes, it is.'

'So a holiday, is it?'

'Yes it is, yes, back dere I'm in property.'

'What property?'

'113b Ethel Road, Kilburn. Have you ever heard of it?'

'No.'

Here the conversation rusted up. Looney lubricated it back to life. 'Der Nilgiri Hills, dat's where they grow tea in der west of India.'

'To be sure.'

'Den dere's der Hanging Gardens of Babylon, Three Tousand B.C.'

'Would youse believe dat?'

'I'm descended from der Kings of Ireland.'

'Der Kings, is it? Dat must ha been a few tousand years ago.'

'Der giant squid is sixty feet long.'

There was another monumental pause, the landlord, his head at right angles to his back, drained his glass. 'Ahhh, now I remember someone sayin' dat right here in Drool. Der Irish King was in a battle with dem Danes.'

75

looney the mighty irish high king stood on a dung mound and called, 'all right, youse danes, i challenge any one of yez small ones to a duel.'

the challenge drew from the ranks of horned warriors a giant monster of a dane smothered in red hair, nineteen feet high, a mass of broken noses, carbuncles and no overtaking signs. throwing aside his shield he strode up the hill, shaking the ground. there was a crash!

as the high king's bottle went, he clapped his hands, his bearer handed him his two-handed sword. 'all right, youse ignorant bloody dane, nilgiri hills, tea-growing area in west india, follow dat.'

the dane did: he gobbed on the turf, he circled the high king, crash! there went the high king's bottle again. the high king warned the dane, 'get out of ireland or we will.'

the dane now advanced straight at king looney who advanced backward down the hill all the while warning the dane, 'annuder step closer an' youse is dead.'

many backward steps later, the dane was still not dead. the high king looney tried a ploy to baffle him. 'the thylacine is extinct in tasmania.' he said. king looney did the ali shuffle and fell over.

'have you hurt yourself?' said the dane.

'no,' said the king.

'good. den get up and fight, you bastard,' said the dane.

looney whirred his sword over his head. 'i'm warning youse,' said king looney, now backing over the ulster border...

'ahduzthisgrabyez' roared the dane and pinned the high king to the wall.

with a flourish of his quill pen, he gave the dane a post-dated cheque. 'let dat be a lesson to you,' he said...

THE SINGER

Garda O'Brien had never wanted to be a policeman. 'Make a man of you,' said his father. No, O'Brien yearned to be the next Mario Lanza. He was better than Lanza, Lanza was dead while he was alive, there the resemblance ended. O'Brien was tall and thin, his voice was tall and thin, nasal and quivery as though he had a clockwork vibrator strapped to his scrotum. He'd sung at police concerts but had never been asked back. Strangely, after every police concert he'd been posted. Only last month he was singing at the police concert in downtown lovely Limerick, now here he was in dreary Drool!

He drew abreast of The Saint and Scholar public house. By now all the exterior drunks had departed belching and spewing into the night. He could hear illegal drinking! He rapped on the door with his truncheon. Inside there was a guilty silence.

'It's der fockin' polis,' slurred a whiskey-sodden voice, and thud! Immediately Rory Mullins drew five pounds from the till then drew two bolts from the door.

'Good mornin',' said O'Brien. 'I know it's St Patrick's day –'

'So do we,' interrupted a drink-strangled voice.

'You are all liable to arrest,' cautioned O'Brien. 'However' – he cleared his throat and after a few vocal mi-mi-mis sang, 'Be my love.'

The captive drunks listened in respectful silence. His head shaking vigorously with vibrato, his little lumpy adam's apple fibrillating at high speed, O'Brien finished. In the deathly silence that followed he said, 'Let *that* be a lesson to you,' and takin the five pounds he left. 'Dat was a near ting,' said Mullins, 'One clap and he'd ha sung all bloody night.'

77

THE FLASHER II

At Kilburn police station Constable Ward was still smarting over the buried dog affair. This was his seventh year in the force without promotion, his wife had nagged him over his failure. 'There's plenty of murders in London,' she said. 'Why can't you catch one? If you can't catch one, *do* one, you'd be better off in the nick.' He tried, he polished the floor outside her bedroom to a high degree of slipperiness, he waxed the bottom of her slippers, he left the cable bare by her bedside lamp, on holiday he took her for a walk along crumbling cliffs, but fate decreed. With the increased activities of the IRA and the PLO in London he thought he'd ask for a transfer to where the action was. And so he arrived in Kilburn in the centre of the Irish community, *this* is where the IRA would be.

The Irish were 'tick', he'd do some investigating on his own account, he listened to Terry Wogan and copied his accent, he hired a black curly wig, he wore a dark blue suit, a white shirt, green tie and brown boots, the uniform the micks wore to recognise each other when drunk. So disguised, he haunted the Irish pubs: 'God bless all in here, long live der Pope,' he'd say, and they would say, 'It's that cunt of an English polis again.'

He kept his eyes open for suspicious parcels. There was that black plastic bag under the pub seat, just in time he had hurled it through the plate-glass window into the street where, on impact, three tins of Kennomeat rolled out. Outside Harrods he had thrust a suspicious brown paper parcel into a bucket of water and thus prevented a pair of expensive brown shoes from exploding. Superintendent Haymes had called him in. 'For God's sake, Ward, will you stop it! Go for something simple, man, like illegal parking, drunks pissing in doorways, flashers and the like.'

Flashing, according to the *Daily Mirror* poll, was one of the ten most popular crimes among elderly women. Which brings us to Frank Chezenko now strolling on the perimeter of the Kilburn and District Nature Club. The club had a unique beginning, it was formed the moment Leon Marks's wife had caught him and the au pair naked on the ironing board, 'Look darling,' the little fat man said, 'I started a nature club for you.' From his savings he'd been forced to buy a derelict garden and solicit new members, who were not long in coming forward. This day a sea of fat white appalling bodies were socialising in the sun: some were playing badminton, male and female appendages flying gaily in all directions; others disported themselves on the sun terrace. There was a huge fat woman with hairs on her fanny like a deserted crow's nest, and a long thin male with a willy that reached to his knee with a curve in it that made it look like a hockey stick with an egg cosy on the end.

Walking along a hedge that hides all this was limping Frank Chezenko. He hadn't had a decent flash since he paid his rent, and now he felt the need. Peering through the hedge, to his delight he saw a group of nude people playing leap frog, ideal! In one bound Chezenko pushed through the hedge and FLASH . . . FLASH . . . FLASH! The recipients were all stunned, women screamed. One whispered, 'Darling!' 'You filthy swine!' said a male with a small one. 'Can I have your business card?' said a lady. Mad with jealousy, the male nudes threw themselves upon the flasher, holding him and his willy down. 'Phone the police!' cried a man. 'Not too quickly,' said a matron.

Constable Ward put down his football coupon to answer the phone. 'Kilburn police station . . . What? A flasher, where? . . . we'll be right over.' He slammed the phone down, smashing it.

The Noddy car bearing Constable Ward drew up at the Nature Club. 'He's in here,' said a naked man.

'Is he still doing it?'

'Yes, there's a big crowd.'

'Leave it to me, sir,' said Ward, pushing past.

'I'm sorry, sir, it's a club rule, no one's allowed in with clothes on.'

Duty first, the policeman stripped and advanced on the luckless Chezenko.

'Let him up,' said the policeman.

Slowly the Hungarian and his crushed willy rose to his feet.

'I'm arresting you for indecency,' said Ward.

'Who are you?' said Chezenko.

'I am a police cons –'

FLASH – FLASH – FLASH.

'Will you stop doing that while I'm talking to you! I'm a police constable and I'm taking you in.'

'Taking me in what?' Chezenko eyed him up and down – not much opposition there. 'How do I know you are a constable, where's your badges of office?' FLASH – FLASH – FLASH – a woman fainted in ecstasy.

Constable Ward ran to his clothing and returned wearing his helmet and blowing a whistle. Thus adorned, he foolishly handcuffed Chezenko's hands in front where he produced further damning evidence of indecent exposure, including the last turkey in the shop. As Ward drove the flasher away he swore he saw women crying.

THE DROOL BUGLE

Desmond McGuinness had been editor and reporter of the *Drool Bugle* for fifty years. His father had been the same before him – he was prematurely retired when a compositor's tray crashed on his head and killed him. 'But fer his death he'd still be alive today,' said McGuinness, who, despite being colour-blind and myopic, had written the copy, done the lay-out and inked the plates. Framed on the office wall were those great past headlines, when Hibernia was aflame with passion blood and bullets, the soul of Ireland was on the English rack.

EAMMON ED VALERR HOLDS OUT AGAINST ENGLISH TROPS!

Irish repubclina army in Actnol!

ENGHLISH ARREST RONG LADDERS!

And that day when Cathleen ni h-Ualain was freed, the streets were awash with Guinness, the headline that meant Liberty:

Trity singed! De Valeridoo declars Repubblick %½$!

This week was another amazing story. The man who had photographed the opening of King Tutankhamen's tomb with its alleged curse, Lawrence Dawson, had died aged ninety-nine and the headline read:

THE CURSE STILL RINGS TRUE!

This morning, short ½ sighted McGuinness "/ 2½ tried to FOcus on his Broiled egg, six times he had aimed violent swings to cut the top off and missed, opposite sat his 1/4@ wife Brede½%$, he said, 'Cann you HelP with this egg½%$.'

Leaning over she deftly sliced off the top, simultaneously putting her hand full in the marmalade, spilt the tea and crashed a plate on to the floor.

'Thrak you dear½%$,' he said.

Brede towered above her spouse by two feet eight inches, the doctor had warned when they married that when they had sex neither would have anybody to talk to. Why had he married such a tall woman? Her raven black hair hung down to her shoulders, her skin was luminous white, her expression one of knowledge and learning, the sensuous cherry lips were made for poetry and song, two Elizabeth Taylor eyebrows arched above a pair of Wedgwood blue eyes full of meaning and intelligence, all this and an idiot.

Local news was hard to come by in Drool, this week's scoop – a pair of red lace knickers found at dawn outside Father Costello's manse! McGuinness lost not a moment, this was the age of the computer. Jumping on his bike he raced to the office, the morning edition had a full front page photo of the garment with the stark headline.

WHOS KNICKERS! SHICK HORROR

Drool, Wednesday
AT DAWN this smornig Garda O'Brien returning from a feet patrol discovered a pair of red knickers outside Father Costello's residence, so fur the Garda are taking no action 4 ××× @ £. Sgt Kelly said, 'We are treating this ass an occi-dent.' When quoshtioned Father Costello said, 'This is what comes from too much wireless.' Magistrate Terence O'Scrotai said, 'There is far too much of this kind of thing harpooning in Drool.' Somewhere in Drool there is a woman workling around wid no knockers, who iss she, how long can she keep gonging? The final wod from the Gardai was, 'Somewhere somEone must know who this-£woman is.'

Reuterrrr

The sensational disclosures had upped the circulation of the *Bugle* from a modest sixty-three to an incredible sixty-seven. What McGuinness didn't know was that across the Irish Sea a pair of tits on Page Three got four million.

THE PRESS INTERVIEW

There was talk in the village of a stranger from the London town who was in property. Was this to be the first of the tourist boom that had been promised this hundred years? McGuinness would see.

Dismounting outside Looney's cottage he pondered how a rich tourist would put up in a condemned cottage with thatch that looked like punk rockers' wigs in a gale. What was *that???* To an aesthete it was an early Dali painting, to a voyeur it was a Peeping Tom, to an optician it looked like conjunctivitis, to a woodpecker it was something to be enlarged, in reality behind frayed curtains, peering through a hole in the cardboard window pane, was the little red eye of Looney. It observed a man on a bike, both long due in the museum. Who was this humpety-backed feller wearing a bowler hat held up by his ears and string bicycle clips? Possibly a yuppy or one of the punk rockers of Drool.

McGuinness knocked with his brolly on the door.

From the keyhole, 'Dere's a cheque in the post.'

Slowly with a hammer behind his back Looney opened the door. Had they followed him over here? So far so good, he thought.

McGuinness raised his bowler, leaving the hat lining still round his head. 'Good morning £%,' he said and handed Looney his card.

'Dere's nuttin' on it,' said Looney.

'It's on the $ other side ½,' said McGuinness.

Looney paused, what a bloody silly place to print it, on the back: 'Desmond McGuinness, Editor, *Drool Bogle*'.

Looney blinked at the card, this could be a trap. 'Is youse a debt collector?' he said, clutching the hammer.

McGuinness smiled, revealing twenty years of inept Irish dentistry. 'No, sir, I am @½ a reporteR.'

Looney dropped the hammer to the floor with a thud.

'I'd like an ½$ interview.'

This is more like it, thought Looney. 'Ah, yes,' he said, diving his hand into his torn pocket to scratch his balls. 'Well, I'm over here [scratch scratch scratch] lookin' up me family ancestors.' He withdrew his hand, letting them swing free.

'Which part ½ do they liVe?'

'Dey don't live anywhere.'

'Why not½?'

'They're dead.'

'Oh, this woulD MIK wonderful copy fOr the *Rdool Bugle* & £ ½ . . . .

OVERSEAs MAN OFF PROPerty IN DrOOL

A VISITER to Drool isMr
Mick Looney, he is heur
locKing £ up his Ancestors.
He Klams he is () descended
Frim the Kings *? of Clare
He aslo/claims THat Giant
s2quids are sixty feet lo
-ng.

Reuter

THE FLASHER III

Prison Chaplin Father Geoff Neasden looked through the spyhole of Chezenko's cell. Chezenko heard the eye-cover being pushed aside, in a trice he was on his feet and FLASH – FLASH – FLASH. Father Neasden recoiled from the spyhole, this man was sick he needed fatherly advice. Neasden inserted the joyless key in the lock and opened the cell door.

FLASH – FLASH – FLASH went the prisoner.

'Not now,' he cautioned. 'Stop that, Frank.'

FLASH – FLASH – FLASH SCREAMMMMMMM. Chezenko had got it caught in the zip.

'See,' said Father Neasden. 'That's God's punishment.'

'No, it's not,' said the prisoner, 'it was bad timing. Being in solitary, I don't get enough practice.'

'Frank,' said Father Neasden, sitting on the bed, 'I'm here to give you God's help.'

'I don't need God's help,' said Chezenko. 'I can manage on my own.' FLASH – FLASH – FLASH. 'There, what's wrong with that?' he said.

Father Neasden had to agree there was nothing wrong with it save it was six inches longer than normal, but then this man was a star in his own right.

'I tell you,' went on Chezenko, 'this is the alternative world's entertainment.'

But who enjoys it?' said Father Neasden.

'I do,' said Chezenko, giving the defeated Father Neasden a few farewell flashes.

To date this prison consisted of decent muggers, robbers and rapists, this man could get the prison a bad name.

THE PHANTOM SINGER

Garda O'Brien sat in deep gloom in his police quarters. He stood up in his underpants and faced the mirror, he wasn't a bad-looking feller. True, his ears did stick out but then so did Clark Gable's, yes, he had a big nose, but so did Barry Manilow, and *he* sang. No, like Van Gogh, he was before his time. After a few tuning mi-mi-mis he sang, 'Ramonaaaa, I'll meet you byeeeee the water fallllllllll-er!' How could they not like his voice? Very well, if they didn't appreciate his singing *he'd* bloody *make* them listen!

A dark Drool night, the last drunks had slid and slobbered their way home to waiting wives who laid them out with frying pans. Along the dark silent cat-haunted streets a figure in full evening dress wearing a terrorist head mask with a top hat skulked in the shadows. With practised stealth he disappeared down an alley only to reappear again, it was a cul-de-sac. Finally, with athletic prowess he vaulted over the fence, falling face down into the garden.

Pausing only to say 'Oh, fuck,' the figure looked up at the back bedroom window. Inside slept Mr and Mrs Sam Gronnivan, both lost in their pensioned-off dreams; vibrating gently to their snores two sets of teeth gradually moved across the dresser. Moving with the grace of a panther the prowling figure placed a ladder against the wall. Upstairs Sam Gronnivan in his sleep muttered, 'The figs, the figs,' turned on his side and tore one off. From outside came a crash as the figure fell from the fifth rung landing with a sickening thud. In a dazed voice he hissed, 'Oh, fuck.' Again the magic of a mystery was everywhere. 'The figs, the figs,' muttered Sam Gronnivan deep in some unrecorded senile dream.

A top-hatted figure appeared framed in the window, silently

he raised the lower sash, first one leg then the other sought purchase inside. He approached the bed and switched on the light. Drawing a .38 pistol loaded with blanks, he fired a shot towards the ceiling. Blinking, gasping, shaking themselves to consciousness, they gasped out their pre-rehearsed lines. 'We are poor Jewish pensioners . . .' It was to be a frightening night for the Gronnivans.

'Don't move,' whispered the phantom pointing the pistol, then sang 'Be my love', and without a pause he went into a Mario Lanza medley. 'Clap, you bastards,' he said to the shivering couple. It was a tortured hour later that the phantom backed out of the window pausing long enough for it to crash down on his fingers.

Screaming 'Oh, fuck,' yet again, he fell off the ladder.

Sergeant Kelly stood in the Gronnivans' kitchen, his back to the range, the seat of his trousers steaming up his jacket, his cap under his arm, in his left hand he held a notepad, in the other an indelible pencil. He wrote down the amazing details of the hooded top-hatted intruder.

'Ohhhh,' groaned Sam Gronnivan, 'it was terrible, terrible, he stood dere pointin' dis pistol at us, right at *us*, dere was the whole room he could have pointed at and he pointed it at *us*.'

'Not so fast, Sam,' said Kelly. 'I don't take the shorthand, how do you spell pistol?' he said.

'P I S T A L,' said Sam.

'I'll put down the gun,' said Kelly. 'Now what happened next?'

Sam went on, he told how this hooded fiend had kept that pistal pointed, then he had *sung* at them! 'He sunged, den he made us clap him. He said if we didn't clap he'd kill himself and then we'd have his death on our conscience.'

Dutifully Sergeant Kelly wrote down '. . . debt on their conscience.'

'Den when we'd finished der clappin',' went on Sam, 'he sunged 'The Desert Song', then the bugger said do youse have a request and me Molly said she'd like 'Danny Boy', so I hit her and still pointin' der gun he sunged dat bloody tune.'

'Oh,' said Kelly, pausing to lick his pencil, leaving an indelible mark on his tongue, 'would you recognise this feller's voice?'

'Oh, yes,' said Sam.

'What was it like?'

'Fockin' terrible,' said Sam.

'I can't write dat down,' said Kelly. 'I can't write down fockin' terrible, can you gis us a different opinion.'

'Yes,' said Sam. 'Fockin' awful.'

Voice, terrible awful, wrote Kelly. 'Could you recognise him again?'

'Oh, yes,' said Sam. 'If he was dressed like dat again, I'd recognise him.'

Kelly put another indelible ink dot on his tongue, which now looked like a leopard. 'Did he take anything of value?' said Kelly.

'No,' said Sam.

'Why do you think that was?' said Kelly.

'Dere was bugger-all of value to take,' said Sam.

'Has you any idea who dis feller was?' said Kelly.

'Yes,' said Sam. 'I had no idea who dis feller was.'

Oh, this was a real interesting case, thought Kelly, he could sell this to the *Drool Bugle*. 'Now, Mrs Gronnivan, have you anything to say?'

Molly Gronnivan looked up from her knitting. 'Yes,' she said. 'He cracked the piss pot.'

Good heavens, thought Kelly, he must have had a powerful stream to do that! 'Did he use the receptacle while he was singing?'

'No,' said Mrs Gronnivan. 'He wasn't dat clever, he tripped on it.'

'Would you like to put a price on the vessel?' said Kelly.

'Oh yes,' said Sam, 'I'd love ter put a price on it.'

So ended Sergeant Kelly's enquiries.

THE LOONEY TO THE CASTLE

It was one of those sunny days when dogs go mad running in circles to catch their tails, and in Ireland they do. Looney rose from his reeking bed, pulled on his trousers, fiddlingly he tied the string round his waist. This gold-shot morning his wife was at Sunday Mass praying the cottage would burn down, preferably with Looney in it. Looney looked in the mirror and screamed, a severe attack of face, a head transplant! *That's* what he needed. After a cup of tealeaves and a piece of carbonised toast, he pulled on his boots, his jacket, his trilby.

Today being the Sabbath, he thought it an ideal day to apply for the job as odd-job man with this landed gentryman. He'd take a short cut across the fields, which was three miles longer. He clambered clumsily over a stile ripping the seat of his trousers on a nail, exposing his scrotum to the elements. To stop them hanging out he lowered his trousers to his hips, and this brought the crotch down to his knees, so he appeared to be tottering along on a pair of dwarf's legs. A mile of perambulating and he halted by a hedgerow for a smoke, he delved into his tin of surviving fag ends and chose a month-old Sweet Afton. Puffing, he lay back in the receiving grass, the warm sun melted what energy he had and he drifted into a shallow unshaven dream . . .

king looney of clare ushered from his battle tent and tore a few royal ones off. 'wave dem away,' he ordered the royal disperser. scattered around were tents of the royal army of clare. the sounds of multiple military snoring filled the soft dawn air. a panting royal equerry, resplendent in green sacking, galloped up on a donkey, dismounted and disappeared up to his neck in a bog. 'yer majesty,' he gasped from ankle level, 'dere's a message from der secret service.' with a loud sucking sound king looney hauled the muck-covered equerry to safety. 'der danes are goin' ter attack at dawn'.

dawn! dat would mean an early breakfast, those danes, bloody clever makin' you fight on a full stomach. 'i'll show 'em, we'll go without breakfast! we'll have breakfast tonight! tell der men, for every pair of danish balls i'll give 'em a nail ter hang 'em on'. he signalled the royal herald. 'sound der alarm.'

the herald raised the cow's horn to his lips, gave a mighty double blast, and ruptured himself. he rolled on the floor. 'oh christ! me groils,' he screamed. they threw him in the river.

'youse lotta bastards,' he yelled as he floated downstream into the irish sea.

the royal soothsayer grovelled at the foot of the royal leather and cow-dung throne. 'ohhhhhhhh,' he groaned as he rolled a handful of bones and crap in his dilly bag. 'ohhhhhhhhhhhhhhhhh,' he went on.

king looney watched him attentively.

'ohhhhhhhhhhhhhh,' groaned the soothsayer.

'fer christ's sake, get on wid it,' said looney.

the soothsayer threw the bones and crap on the floor. 'ohhhhhhhhhhhhhh,' he continued, and as he could think of nothing else said, 'ohhhhhhhhh' again. agitating the bones and crap he stood bolt upright and with a look of horror on his face pointed a forecasting trembling filthy finger at the floor. he sucked in air in a dreadful inhaling whistle and said, 'ohhhhhhhhhhhhhhhhhhhhh.'

'youse bastards,' he said as he, his bones and crap drifted down the river…

the day of the battle dawned, the army stood to arms. 'from der right number,' said the captain.

from the serried ranks they shouted off, 'one, twelve, five hundred and fifty-nine,'

'all correct and present,' said the captain.

'where are der edder five hundred and ninety-seven?' said king looney.

'pissed off, sire.'

'men of clare,' said the king, 'der danes are coming. if dere's more than three of dem we're pissin' off too! udderwise we stand an' fight. any questions?'

spearman mcmoon took one pace forward. 'wot about our wages?' he said.

'you bastards,' he screamed as he floated down the river.

from a tree a lone irish crow called crippin watched from a nest that looked like the hairs on a woman's fanny. in the distance

he could see a hundred roistering danish men-at-arms nearing
the camp. their leader, vung the terrible, approached the irish
king's tent and set fire to it. from inside came a choking scream, a
man smouldering in pyjamas and a tin crown rushed out, smoke-
blackened with singed eyebrows.

'who dun dat,?' raged king looney. he espied the giant figure of
the danish leader. christ!!! from now, no one would accept looney's
laundry.

vung pointed at his men-at-arms now surrounding the irish
camp.

'youse don't frighten an irish king dat easily,' said looney and
gobbed in defiance straight in vung the terrible's eyes. 'youse
bastards,' shouted king looney as he and his army of three drifted
down the river...

The afternoon drew on, a sensuous heat swam over the
lilting meadows, Looney stirred in his rent trousers. About
this time a pure-bred little Irish bull ant called Powell also
stirred inside Looney's trousers. The little ant wandered freely
inside his trousered cave. What was this thing hanging down?
The little ant's jaws snapped close. From above rose a wailing
scream as Looney had lift off and clutched his willy dislodging
Powell.

'Oh, Jesus, wot's dat?' he said. Inspecting his parts to find a
growing red spot on the end, for a moment he panicked. Was
it AIDS? A snake? He could never get down there to suck the
poison out . . . he'd have to find a dwarf.

Sounds of a galloping horse. One approached carrying a
bowler-hatted rider. Lord Chatsworth of Drool reined the
horse to a halt, towering over the still-traumatised Looney
standing with his nipped willy in his hand!

Lord Chatsworth cracked his whip. 'How *dare* you expose
yourself on my land!'

'I'm not exposin' meself, I'se just been bitten on me cock.'

Lord Chatsworth cracked his whip – crack, crack. 'Ow!' he
screamed as it caught his own ear. 'Get off my land' he raged.

'Your land?' said Looney.

'*My* land!' said Chatsworth, standing in the stirrups,
collapsing one.

'Who said it's your land,' said Looney.

91

'I fought for it,' said Chatsworth.

'OK, I'll foit you for it,' said Looney.

The little bull-ant, recovered from his airborne journey, found himself in the horse's groin, just a little taste. With a screamed whinny the horse reared and with the whip-cracking-hanging-on-for-grim-death-one-leg-hanging-down raced away, with his rider crying, 'My land, get off my land!' gradually getting off it himself. The horse cleared a hedge into the field containing Sherbert the virile stud stallion. Soon Chatsworth was crushed to the saddle, his bowler hat jammed over his eyes as he concertinaed up and down between two horses. 'Anybody want to buy my land?' he screamed.

THE CASTLE BOURNE

Castle Bourne, the medieval monolithic pile, loomed over the Drool landscape like a giant crouching granite beast. Built by Dragh Na Molloy, the great Irish chief, to protect himself from the bailiff, it had been passed down as Molloy after Molloy slaughtered each other until the area ran out of them. It lay empty these two hundred years, its belfry upside down with bats, its eaves full of pigeons, starlings and dreams.

Then Lord O'Goldstein OBE, had bought it. Too big for his own uses, he let the other half of fifty rooms to the Aga Kuka, an Indian potentate and racehorse breeder. Behind him were the great stud stables.

His downfall had been a basement room in Soho run by Miss Muriel Body, a strict disciplinarian and relief masseuse. There he was enjoying innocent fun with convivial company, he paid her a hundred pounds to let him sit nude inside a Victorian cupboard feeling a jelly and looking through the keyhole. Now, who was that forty-two-year-old square-jawed man with a cavalry moustache, a pale pink lipstick, mauve eyeshadow, wearing a transparent body corset, white fishnet stockings over bandy legs and red peek-a-boo stiletto hells and bad typist? Of course! It was Donald Martin, manager of the Nat West at Croinge. Tonight was Hollywood Stars Night. There was bearded Queen's Counsel Norrish Lumps, who'd come as Rita Hayworth, what lucky person would get him? And who was that in the cage dressed as a vicar and wanking? Why, it was Mr Crick from the Wandsworth and Wembley Building Society. So it was really bad luck when Inspector Dick Haymes and his crude vice squad burst in.

So sad, O'Goldstein was a man of breeding, mostly Rhode Island Red chickens. He made his fortune with battery hens, gave money to one of the top ten charities and was given an OBE, thus putting the royal seal of approval on cruelty. Another donation to a media-orientated charity and he was knighted, finally Queen's Birthday Honours, bingo! A donation to the Cancer Fund and a resulting lordship; like justice, charity should be done but, most important, be *seen* to be done. Somewhere in London a Mr and Mrs Ted Baines of modest means fostered three homeless children on very little money, no birthday honours for them, what they needed was Saatchi & Saatchi.

This afternoon Lord O'Goldstein sat naked in his giant castle bedroom massaging a jelly and dreaming of keyholes. The money still rolled in from his assault and battery chicken farms. While he rattled round giant empty rooms, his chickens lived in cruel crushed confinement, three to a cage, not for them the sun, not for them a simple walk or stretching their wings. Daily their product was eaten by millions of unthinking morons, all subscribing to a cruelty that would one day indict this century as barbaric.

Apart from jelly-massaging, O'Goldstein had another dark secret – Jeremy his black illegitimate son, an amiable lunatic with a penchant for dressing up. Today it was Quasimodo.

This duo were supervised by Mrs Drusilla Fitts, the sixty-year-old lesbian housekeeper/cook, giving occasional relief massage. She stood six foot, shaped like a phone box and just as out of order. She wore voluminous billowing black clothes that made her look like a coal barge under full sail, she stalked the dark dank granite-grey corridors, most of the time totally lost, the heavy castle keys jangling round her waist giving a clanking clue to her whereabouts.

Ignorant of all this, Looney walked innocently through the portcullis and approached the massive forecourt door. He tugged at the bellpull and pulled it out of its socket. Behind the door he heard the bell fall off the wall and hit the floor.

The door opened and a crouched black figure with a humpety back appeared. 'Sanctuary – sanctuary!' it cried.

Jasus! A crippled nigger!

It was immediately yanked to one side and a nude

94

O'Goldstein wearing a capel and carrying a jelly appeared. 'Take no notice of him,' he said. 'He's not well.'

Looney eyed the nude man. 'Is youse a nudist colony?'

'No, I'm Lord O'Goldstein, what do you want?'

'I'se told dat youse were looking for a handyman.'

'Oh, do you like jelly, my boy?'

'Well, yes.'

'What colour?'

'Oh, any one, all colours taste much the same to me.'

O'Goldstein beckoned him in. Looney followed the naked man, he didn't like this.

'It's very hot today,' said Lord O'Goldstein.

Looney followed him upstairs, the bare Jewish bum going ahead. He was possibly one of de eccentric millionaires, thought Looney.

O'Goldstein led him into a large library, giant windows gave a view to the distant hills of Drool and the stud farm. He backed into a creaking rocking chair and placed a plate of jelly on his lap.

'Now,' said Lord O'Goldstein.

'Now what?' said Looney.

'Let me finish, man – now! What are your credentials?'

Looney explained he'd been in the army.

What rank did he rise to?

'I rose to private.'

'Are you a handy man?'

'Oh, yes.'

'For instance?'

'For instance, I'm a handy man.'

So it went on.

His Lordship realised that this man was a cut above the others, so he could see how bad things were in Drool.

'Now,' said O'Goldstein starting to rock back and forth with increasing vigour, 'can you make jelly?'

'Oh yes, I can make jelly.'

'You know a jelly has to be kept in a cool place.'

'Ireland's a cool place.'

'Good,' he said with great emotion. 'I like a different colour

95

jelly each day.' With increased momentum he rocked back and forth. 'Say red jelly,' he said.

'Red jelly,' said Looney.

'Ohhhhhhh,' cried O'Goldstein in ecstasy rocking his chair past its point of balance shooting O'Goldstein backwards, a loud thud as the Jewish head hit the marble floor. He lay quite still as the jelly rolled off his lap.

Straining, Looney lifted the chair upright only to see O'Goldstein slide forwards on to the floor again. Looney leaned over the supine Lord. 'Ups-a-daisy,' encouraged Looney, a lot of bloody good.

'What's going on in here?'

Looney turned to see Mrs Fitts steaming down on them.

'Where's his jelly?' she said sternly.

'Underneath him,' said Looney.

'Who put it there?' she said.

'He fell on it.'

A woman of action, she knelt and raised the lord's head in her lap. 'Quick, the brandy,' she said and pointed to the decanter.

Hurriedly Looney poured out a good medicinal measure and handed it to the woman.

'Cheers,' she said and downed it in one gulp. 'He's looking better already,' she said.

'So do you,' said Looney.

The inert figure stirred. 'Ohh,' it groaned. 'Where am I?' he said.

'Here,' said Looney.

'Don't just stand there,' she rapped, so Looney sat down. 'You fool,' said Mrs Fitts. 'Help me get him on to the couch.'

Looney took the lolling head, Mrs Fitts took his lolling ankles; together they slid him across the room on his red jelly, straining to lift the inert body on to the couch. Ping! The string on Looney's trousers snapped bringing them down round his ankles. Grabbing at the garment Looney let go of his lordship's head which hit the floor for the thud time. Filled with compassion, Mrs Fitts downed another brandy.

THE STALLION ROBBERY

The great stallion Sherbert pranced and whinnied in his clover-strewn paddock, his owner the Aga Kuka lay upstairs prancing and whinnying on top of sweet Rosie O'Day.

'Of course I love you,' he said in his sing-song Hindu voice.

'Then why don't you marry me?' she gasped between thrusts.

'Ohhh no, that is against my religion, the great book of the Bhagavadgita says no Hindu must marry a Christian.'

Rosie couldn't get it clear. A Hindu could fuck the arse off a Christian, but marriage no.

'Oh, no,' went on the Aga, 'our relationship is a secret of two lovers that must never be released into the outer world of the Swamis.' And all that balls.

As the Aga Kuka plunged away at his Celtic maiden, his moneywinner the prancing proud stallion Sherbert was being observed through the Celtic bushes by two pairs of eyes, in Ireland that made three, the Prune brothers: the one-eyed Rory, and Tige, both men bereaved of late by the death of their donkey – without him their business of selling peat ground to a halt. For a time they got Drool village idiot Jasper McQuonk to pull it, but he was stricken with piles. At this moment he lay face downwards on his bed, his mother applying a hot bread poultice to them while he screamed, 'No butter.'

Penniless, the Prunes debated how to save the business, they had always stolen their donkeys, it was a family tradition, but this was the age of the computer! Why steal a donkey, why not a horse? This brought them to their vantage point with the 'stuff'. Drool chemist, James Coughlan had told them, 'This will tranquillise anybody.' How were the Prunes to know

97

that, with failing eyesight, Coughlan had given them a hypodermic of the powerful stimulant Benzocaine?

Tippy-toe and shushing loudly, the Prunes approached one end with a carrot, at the other end Tige injected the fluid into the animal's rump. Coughlan had said it would 'take a while to act'. It was long enough for them to harness the stallion to their farm cart. Inside the great stallion the stimulant started to take hold. Well pleased, Rory Prune said, 'Gee up, horsey.' All three disappeared.

It was James Coughlan himself who first heard it, a frenzied sound of a horse approaching at great speed, galloping, whinnying, and the rattle of a farm cart falling to pieces and two white-faced blurred men shouting, 'Woah, fer Christ sake, woah!' It shot past his chemist shop in the soft morning light and disappeared up Drool High Street heading south in a cloud of dust, only to reappear ten minutes later going north with the cart going west.

'Fer Christ sake, woah,' screamed Rory.

'Hail Mary full of grace, make the bugger stop!' chanted Tige, as the speeding shuddering ensemble raced towards the Clare–Galway border.

Along the lovely shores of Lough Derg they galloped. Neither of the Prune brothers seemed the slightest interested in the magnificent passing scenery, nor the Japanese who photographed them. On and on galloped the frenzied frothing stallion.

In a death-like grip, Rory hung on to the reins, his face a mask of fear, his trousers full of it, crash! 'Der fockin' back's fallen off!' screamed Tige as the maniacal palfrey headed up the road towards the beautiful Slieve Aughty Mountains.

Soon the brothers were breathing the delightfully pure air at three thousand feet. The American tourists saw them from their Daimler. 'Look, Wilbur, how cute, an Irish jaunting cart,' said one and waved gaily after them.

This is too good to miss, thought the mighty Sherbert spotting a delightful brood mare grazing contentedly in a field. Soon the contented mare was shuddering as the great thrusting stallion set about producing a new Curragh winner.

98

The Prunes saw a moment of opportunity. 'Quick, get the harness off the bugger,' shouted Rory, leaping to the ground. In a frenzy Tige grabbed the headset and tried to wrestle it off. Too late! Too late! The stallion, well pleased, with a two-foot-long phallus hanging down, reared up with a cheerful neigh.

'Fer God's sake, look out!' said Rory, clambering on to the cart. 'He's off again.'

Tige clawed his way back on to the fast-disintegrating cart as the steaming stallion lashed out with its back legs, shattering the buck board, leaving Rory's legs now dangling free. With that the animal bolted out of the field, the cart hurtling up and down over the furrows.

'Woohhhhhh,' said Rory in a despairing voice, this was no way to run a peat business. The worst was to come. The noble stallion in many respects was like any other horse, splat! The dung hurled backwards full in the white face of Rory, Tige getting it second-hand in the neck. 'You dirty bugger!' screamed the Prunes. Mrs O'Driscoll raced out to scoop up the dung for her roses.

At a quiet country crossroads a lone Garda waved on the approaching cart. It ran over him. 'Stop!' yelled the flattened hoof-printed policeman.

The hunter's moon fawned over the sleepy heavy-thatched roofs of Drool, the balm-laden air wafted up the nostrils of the sleeping community, the nocturnal hormones of the cats stirred in their silken bodies. They now crouched on rooftop and garden wall yeowling face-to-face feline poetry. From the quiet distant night came a hollering and a galloping, the Prune brothers and their hurtling cart, louder and louder it thundered through Drool. In the ear of Mick Looney he thought he heard it all and he pondered why anybody would be working so hard at this time of night.

On board the careering cart Rory called above the hiatus to his brother, 'Try and get some fockin' sleep.' On, on and away raced the stallion.

THE DREAMING LOONEY

A summer night over Drool, a crepuscular mist haunted the valley, free-standing cows loomed in the blue-grey mist, the silence only broken by the occasional moo. Sentinel on silver wet boughs, barn owls ululated chilling sepulchral calls, fear-ridden mice scampered through damp grasses to lodge their tremulous bodies in safe coverts. Around opened-mouth warrens rabbits tensed with listening ears, nibble hurry sweet grasses. From some secret somewhere a cricket broadcasted his mating song.

Through the window of his bedroom, sandwiched between laundry-craving sheets, watching the scimitar moon rucking amid racing clouds, lay crapulent Looney, ah, dat selfsame moon must ha shone on me ancestors . . .

King Looney in his cow dung and mud hut lay resplendent on his sacking-covered couch when he awoke. He had been dreaming he was sleeping. Outside, the fire flamed and sang scorching scarlet songs. In a circle sat Looney's courtiers.

Suddenly, after a quick massage of Guinness and potato peelings, King Looney appeared in the doorway, even in those distant days a magnificent dresser. Such taste, a green and purple striped shirt with the London Irish Rugby Club logo on the pocket, a lovely lemon and red spotted tie, a weather- and draughtproof ankle-length saffron kilt bought from the Scotch House costing over two pounds, white woollen football hose like Danny Blanchflower used to wear, patent leather dance pumps as worn by David Jacobs on 'Come Dancing'. A black bowler hat with a gold crown around the hatband like Elton John, completed the ensemble. In his right hand the royal regalia, a rolled umbrella like Steed in 'The Avengers', around his waist on a piece of knotted string hung the royal shillelagh, the ten notches in the handle a reminder of ten great hidings he'd taken from the Danes. He clapped his hands, 'I call the court minstrel to regale us with a heroic poem of great deeds.'

Rising from his tree stump the court minstrel macgonigal stood in the firelight and struck a chord on the harp.

'ohhhhhhhhhhhhhhhhh,' he commenced.

'twas in the year nine oh eight
the terrible danes were approaching at a great rate.
the natives said, 'oh dear, oh dear,
we think the buggers are coming here'
one mick said, 'shall we stand and fight?'
'fuck you,' they said, and ran out of sight.
one was mick looney, a future king.
he said, 'i think there's going to be fighting.'
when the terrible danes came into view
they all ran away except one or two
shouting, 'we are outnumbered a hundred to one!'
those were bad odds so they started to run.
the danes came with rape and pillage,
until then it had been a quiet little village.
they ate the food and drank the wine
and raped the women in extra time.
said looney the future king,
'look here, we don't like this sort of thing.'
that night the danes all sailed away,
they'd had a very enjoyable day.

'you bastards,' shouted macgonigal, as he floated down the river.

Next morning, after his triumphant brush with the Danes, Looney was in a good mood, and a great idea came to him. He smiled a smile that was like sunrise over a sewage farm. A seance! *Dat* might unlock the secret of his ancestry.

THE SEANCE

Mrs Delores Fruit, Drool's only living spiritualist, moved in silent septuagenarian smoothness across the lino of her seance room, her grey hair tied in a huge bun like her head was being inflated. She was rubbing her hands together producing a noise like sandpaper. Behind her followed the cottage loaf form of Mrs Aida Higgins. It was that bugger her husband she wanted to contact, seven years ago he had left home, the bugger! Till then he had given her three years of blissful married life, followed by ten of misery. She had never forgiven him, the bugger! Always moaning that he felt faint, the bugger! And that final disgrace, why had she married an illiterate, subnormal farmhand? Oh, that terrible disgrace, himself caught screwing a cow! The bugger! That court case, the disgrace! That counsel for the prosecution, what he said! 'M'lud, ladies and gentlemen of the jury, on the day of the alleged offence my client was grazing contentedly in a field . . .' The bugger! It was the night she had hit him with a flat iron, he had left on a stretcher, just like that, the bugger! Not so much as a kiss-me-arse he left, never even said goodbye, just laying there with his head split open, the ungrateful bugger.

'So, Mrs Higgins,' purred Mrs Fruit, 'you wish to contact your dear husband.'

Mrs Higgins nodded. 'Yes,' she said through pursed lips like a chicken's bum.

'Please,' said Mrs Fruit, indicating a chair.

Mrs Higgins lowered her vast bulk onto it blotting it from human view.

Mrs Fruit sat silently in her seance chair, drawing a small lace handkerchief from a dilly-bag. Birdlike she placed it delicately to her nose and gave a blast like the Queen Mary, at the same time dislodging her canary from his perch. 'Now,' she said very quietly, 'it's a pound for the first seance, thereafter fifty pee a session.'

Mrs Higgins delved in her bag. One pound, so that's what the bugger was costing her, that bugger! She handed the trembling note across the table to the medium.

'Now,' said Mrs Fruit, 'please concentrate.' With fluttering lids she closed her eyes, grabbed the arm of the chair, threw back her head. 'Ahhhtishoo!' she roared, releasing a shower of dandruff. The dazed canary shook himself and climbed up the ladder again. For the second time Mrs Fruit composed herself. Had it been Debussy he would have committed suicide. 'When we contact dear husband, is there any question you want to ask him?'

Mrs Higgins nodded. 'Yes, ask him what he's done with the bloody fish knives.'

Mrs Fruit shuddered, ask him what he's done with the bloody fish knives. Suddenly Mrs Fruit went limp like a sack of it, then stiffened like rigor mortis. 'Is there anybody there?' she moaned.

'I am,' said Mrs Higgins.

Mrs Fruit tried again. 'Is anybody there in the beyond?'

There followed a long teasing silence. Mrs Higgins leaned forward, the bugger wasn't answering!

Again Mrs Fruit moaned, 'Are you there, Sean Higgins, are you there?'

There came an impact sound as an excessively hairy tom cat shot through the cat flap carrying a wriggling rat in its jaws.

'Mary Mother of God!' screamed Mrs Higgins. Forgetting she had no knickers on, she hoisted her skirts up to her waist. With a fanny that looked like Bernard Shaw, she leapt on to a chair. It collapsed sending her crashing down on the unfortunate pussycat. With a pained yeowl like elastic, it pulled itself from under her pneumatic bulk and galloped out the cat flap leaving the rat free. With hands waving, Mrs Higgins shrieked anew and fled the building.

Outside, Looney, about to enter, was knocked flat by a huge

woman naked from the waist down rushing past. She ran down the street with her Bernard Shaw. Looney watched the cheeks of her bum like alternating jellies.

Inside the seance room, Mrs Fruit stood on her chair watching the rodent seeking a way to escape. This was the worst seance since that one in World War Two. She was working in the WVS in Florence serving tea an' buns to our poor boys from the front. To keep her hand in the spiritual world she held seances for the soldiers to help 'entertain' them. That night when four totally ignorant Royal Artillery gunners agreed to attend they sat around the table baffled.

'Would any of you like to contact any of your loved ones?'

Gunner Robson grunted, 'Yer, I'd like ter contact my muvver Rose.'

Mrs Fruit called to the beyond, 'Hello, Rose Robson . . . hello, Rose Robson, are you there?' she moaned.

What Robson hadn't told her was that his mother was alive and well and living in Brighton. 'She won't hear you from 'ere,' he said.

That was all past. Right now, Looney was calling down the hall, 'Is anybody dere?'

From within came a female voice, 'Helpppppppppppppppppppppppppp!' by which time Looney reached the room. 'The rat,' instructed Mrs Fruit. 'Get rid of the rat!'

Grabbing the creature by the tail, Looney hurled it into the garden.

'I'm sorry about this,' she said.

'Wus dat your rat?' said Looney.

She held her hand up as though she couldn't speak. When Looney showed her a pound she recovered and indicated a chair which Looney placed over the ruins of Mrs Higgins' chair. 'I want ter get in touch wid me ancestors,' he explained.

'Any particular one?' she said.

'Yes,' said Looney, 'any particular one.'

Mrs Fruit told him after the pound it would be another fifty pee. Diving down he pulled fifty pee from his jockstrap. She took it along with a handful of pubic hair.

The medium closed her eyes. Looney watched transfixed,

104

dis must be a powerful woman, anyone who could make Mrs Higgins run down the street naked from the waist down showing her Bernard Shaw must have the power.

'Ohhhhhhhh,' moaned Mrs Fruit. 'Are any of Mick Looney's ancestors there?' Her words hung in the air, she took a deep asthmatic breath. Suddenly she stiffened. 'I have somebodyyyyyyyyyy,' she intoned.

Looney craned forward, the moment of truth. 'What does he say?' he said.

The answer came clear and strong. 'The fish knives are with Aunty Peggy' . . . It was that bugger.

THE DEPARTED

The rain, oh the rain, ever so gentle it fell on man and beast, but most of all it fell on John Collins. Working quietly through the Drool day it dripped generously on to his exposed neck, then, using his spine as a drain, trickled down his back collecting in his underpants dampening his swonnicles. But what was rain after all? Just a dry day with water. It was good to have work in these days of unemployment, especially outdoors with a regular turnover. What could be happier than dealing with people, every day somebody different. He smiled, threw another shovelful up and climbed out of the grave. He paused on the edge to roll a cigarette. As he lit it, the muddy edge collapsed pitching him back into the grave striking his head on the shovel and rendering him unconscious.

Mick Looney entered the graveyard. Were there any Looneys buried here? He walked among the departed, wait, what was this? Jasus! Dere was a body at der bottom of dis grave, no coffin and not filled in, a pauper's grave! Poor devil, he couldn't have been dead long, his fag was still alight. He crossed himself, why not, he'd crossed everybody else, poor devil. The least he could do would be to fill it in, how lucky, here was a shovel.

Dedicatedly he intoned a Hail Mary and he started to shovel in the earth. Good God! As the first clod hit the body it groaned! Or was it his imagination? No, it wasn't his imagination groaning, it was the corpse. The eyes opened, spitting out mud it spoke, 'Wot in Christ name are you doin' man?' it said.

'Oh, I'm sorry, mister, I thought youse wus dead, what are you doin' den, practising?'

The corpse rose again from the dead and pulled itself from the grave.

Oh God, thought Looney, dat was a near ting. 'Tell me, is dere any graves in dis churchyard wid der name Looney?'

Collins thought. 'Ah yes, in that corner dere's a Looney.'

Yes, there in faded Gothic engraving:

𝔗𝔥𝔬𝔪𝔞𝔰 𝔏𝔬𝔬𝔫𝔢𝔶, born 1600, nearly died 1666,

really died 1676

What a discovery! If dis stiff was wearin' a crown it would prove his royal blood!

A hauntingly basalt black banshee-ridden night. From some secret somewhere a dog fox yeowled across the scape to his mate, in the damp air a nightingale sneezed and fell off. It was wet sticky work, down and down scooped the two ghoulish labouring shovels.

'How in Christ's name do they get out of all dis on Judgement Day,' said Looney wiping his brow.

Collins paused in his digging and smiled. Had not this eccentric millionaire given him 50p to help dig up his ancestor? He'd put many a stiff down, this was the first time he'd brought one up again. It made a refreshing change, job-enrichment the Americans called it. A splintering thud as Collins' shovel hit the coffin lid.

'Dat's it,' shouted Looney gleefully.

'Shhhhhhhhhhhhhhhhhh,' warned Collins, sending a shower of spit straight into Looney's face. 'Not so loud, somebody might hear us!'

What was he talking about? No bodies in this yard would ever hear anybody again! With trembling hands Looney pulled the rotten lid off. If this stiff was wearin' a crown . . . The stiff wasn't wearing anything, not even skin. All there was clenched in the skeleton fist was a piece of parchment inscribed, 10 to 1 Dublin Lad. 10 to 1? thought Looney. Why would someone want to write the time on a piece of paper, especially a stiff?

*

107

thomas looney 1600-1676 lay on his deathbed. even worse, he was dying as well. forty years of drinking had paid off. his liver had floated away followed by his kidneys, stomach and intestines. he was now hollow. looney lay still, a beatific smile on his unshaven face. he hummed a little tune.

'he's only got two days to live,' whispered physician mucks.

'can he have a last drink?' said mrs looney.

'no,' whispered the physician, 'that would kill him. however, it won't kill me,' and downed the glass in one gulp. 'i'll see him in the morning,' he whispered.

'yes, but will he see you?' said mrs looney.

the room echoed to the sound of the physician's donkey cart driving away.

looney 1600-1676 sat up in bed, forty-eight hours to live!

'the last will and testament,' he wrote. 'fuck the lot of yer, signed thomas looney.' forty-eight hours to live, he poured a measure of poteen...

thirty-six hours to live! hurriedly he poured out a pint of poteen...

only twenty-four hours to live! he drained the bottle and waited...

sixteen hours to live... he'd have to hurry! a bottle and a half gurgled down the dying man's 1600-1676 throat...

eight hours left, just time for another bottle...

seven, six, five, four, hours and two bottles, three, two, one hours, goodbye!

fifty-nine hours, now he'd been dead eleven hours and another bottle and a half.

the mortician benedict arrived. 'jasus, thomas,' he said, 'not dead yet? look at the time, man!'

looney 1600-1676 sat up and drained the bottle. 'i'm doin' me best, cheers!'

physician mucks shook his head and paused, but still kept charging. 'i don't know what's keeping him alive,' he whispered.

'i think it's the poteen,' said mrs looney.

'then you must keep it away from him or he'll never bloody die!' whispered mucks. 'i'll just take these six bottles for analysis.'

'i got the coffin outside,' said the mortician.

'bring it in den, i won't have so far to go,' said looney.

'what a fine powerful death box dat is,' said mrs looney as in staggered benedict with it on his back. 'it's fockin' heavy as well,' he said, sliding it to the floor.

'is dat fer me?' said looney 1600-1676, his face alight with happiness.

benedict removed the lid showing the pink satin lining, 'i can't keep this coffin waiting much longer,' he warned. 'there's other people waiting to die. how long are you going to hang on?'

mrs looney had a fine idea, why didn't looney himself get in the coffin then invite the neighbours for viewing?

'by gor! dis is more comfortable dan me bed,' said looney, lying back in the padded interior. "tis a grand fit, I tink I'll practise foldin' me arms.'

'twas a grand evening, the peat fire glowing, perfuming the room and looney himself sitting up in his coffin singing with the neighbours and creditors sitting around. 'oh looney boy, youse will make a real fine stiff,' said one.

neighbour dan dillon stood up, eighty-six, straight as a die, as fit as a fiddle, never seen a doctor in his life. 'do you mind if I try dat coffin?' he said.

'der pleasure is mine,' said looney, getting out.

dan dillon lowered himself into the waiting coffin. 'how does that look?' he said. they gave him a burst of applause. dan waved them away. 'oh 'tis nothin',' he said modestly.

'dan, you look better in it than looney,' said his wife.

'wid coffins as good as dat, dyin' will never go out of fashion,' said looney.

'oh yes,' said dan. 'I'm only sorry dat it's not meself dat's goin' ter snuff it.' more applause.

'try closin' yer eyes, dan,' said the wife.

what a good idea, thought dan. shutting his eyes tight, he lay back. 'jasus, dis is like der real ting,' he said to another burst of applause and cries of 'good old dan'.

tears came to the eyes of mortician benedict, this was a great night for coffins.

dan dillon was suddenly quiet, for he, eighty-six, straight as a die, fit as a fiddle, never seen a doctor in his life, died. it was many bottles later before they realised that dear dan dillon had not passed out but on. 'leave him till the morning and see if it wears off,' said the departing mrs dillon. the guests stumbled out into the cloying dark night and compassed towards their homes leaving the trainee corpse with a real one.

'ah dan, man,' said looney 1600-1676, draining the bottle, 'youse don't know wot youse is missin'.'

by morning light physician mucks leaned over the body of dillon. 'this man is dead or he's a brilliant mimic,' he whispered.

the bible says, 'death comes like a thief in the night', but not in this house.

THE PRUNES COME TO A HALT

Clontarragh village is eighty miles from Drool as the crow flies, but then people round here didn't travel by crow, they were into legs. That bird-blessed morning, legs were carrying the villagers about their business.

From the distance a cloud of dust on four legs and three eyes was approaching. From inside came shouting, screaming, neighing and galloping, from out of the dust appeared something that had once been a cart. It was being pulled at incredible speed by what looked like an insane horse frothing at the mouth and occasionally lashing out with its rear legs. Hanging on to the reins was a terrified driver screaming, 'Fer fok's sake, woahhhhhhhhhhhhhhhh.' Behind, in the kneeling position, was another man. With one hand he hung on to the side, with the other he held his holy beads and at a gibbering speed was attempting to say the rosary.

''Tis the Prune brothers,' said some. 'It must be an express delivery.' The horse and cart raced and racketed through the village street, scattering chickens, goats, sheep, children, it even scattered Mrs O'Dowd.

Through the life-long weary day the galloping trio sped across Clare in a giant homing circle, seventeen villages were treated to the spectacle.

'Jasus,' said Rory. What luck! They were actually nearing the Prune brothers' farm. 'As he goes past, jump fer yer fockin' life,' yelled Rory.

Like some biblical miracle the racing stallion suddenly pulled to a screeching halt, spread his rear legs and commenced a long steaming equine micturition that flooded the road and a little Irish ant called Norman carrying a twig to a party. Rory saw a moment of salvation. Leaping from the shattered cart, he picked up a wayside rock and bounced it on the stallion's forehead. With a throttled whinny the great horse crashed unconscious to the road, its tongue hanging out.

'Get me out,' shouted Tige, now trapped underneath the horse. 'Me legs,' he said, 'me legs.' Taking him under the armpits, Rory gave a giant heave. 'Dat's it! I'm comin',' said Tige. One last great longgg heave and Rory pulled his brother free, yes free. Why should he charge him?

Tige stood minus his shoes, socks and trousers. 'Oh Christ, look at dat,' said Tige kneeling down and trying to plunge his arm under the horse. 'Dose are me best trousers!' he moaned. The morning sun shone radiant on his bare bum. Ah, Ireland was still a land of romance.

THE INSPECTOR ARRIVES

Chief Inspector McTruss from the Limerick Garda drove his 1939 car into the forecourt of the Aga Kuka's stud farm. Gently he braked and the mudguard fell off. This would be his most important assignment since that terrible drunken driving charge, luckily he had got off with a caution. Sherbert the great stallion had been stolen! The *whole* horse had gone!

Parking the car he eased a stomach bulging with boiled bacon, potatoes, Irish stew with extra dumplings, Lea and Perrins sauce, four slices of bread and butter, a double helping of blancmange, prunes and custard, three cups of tea and two double brandies, from under the steering wheel. It was like moving a restaurant. With a swivelling motion he got his little short thin legs hanging out of the car, then with a lurch got the rest of himself out. He was a detective of the old school, as so far they hadn't built a new one. A man of action, he immediately photographed the stables, every clue counted! That and memory! Fingerprints! Observation! and *punctuality*! He had told the Aga that he would arrive on Monday punctually at eleven. He looked at his watch, dead on eleven o'clock! On a Tuesday. It was all that changing from winter to summer time.

First, a photograph of himself shaking hands with the Aga Kuka, every clue counted! Next, cross-question the stable lad. 'I want a complete description of the horse.' What? four legs, a tail ... this case wasn't going to be easy, but first a photograph of himself questioning the lad, every clue counted. The trainer gave a *vital* clue, the horse was brown, that meant black, white, grey and piebald horses were no longer under suspicion. McTruss continued, 'What time was the horse stolen?'

'Night time, sorr.'

'Yes, but what time by the clock?'

'I can't tell the time, sorr, I can only tell the calendar, sorr.'

'Then for Christ's sake tell me.'

'It was a Monday, sorr.'

Good! Better have a photograph of himself shaking hands with him saying Monday, every clue counted! Now, one of himself alone pointing at the stable, one with the door open, now another with it closed, now what was his next move? His next move was to step in some horse shit.

Chief Inspector McTruss cast his trained eye over the paddock, a mass of hoofprints! Either it was *one* horse who did a lot of running about, or a lot of horses standing still. In his notebook he recorded, 'There is only one entrance to the stables.' The next sentence he underlined, '*That's where they get in!*'

Since the sensational robbery of the horse the Aga Kuka had been receiving many threatening phone calls. 'Stop fucking my daughter,' was one of them. The Aga had received a long mysterious parcel containing a hoofed leg with the message 'Pay the ransom or this horse will never run again!' Ah ha! thought McTruss, this narrows it down to three-legged brown horses, there couldn't be many of them about! With things as they were it was *imperative* he stayed with the Aga, he was skint.

'This is my manservant Mashi Shitzu,' the Aga introduced McTruss to a smiling shortsighted Nip creep. 'I werry preased to meet yo,' he said. 'This way, preese.' He led McTruss to a sumptious bedroom. 'You rike?'

Yes, McTruss riked it werry much. East is east and west is west and never the twain shall meet, except in Ireland.

Proudly Shitzu announced, 'Me black belt.'

Proudly McTruss replied, 'Me brown braces.'

'No, no,' said Shitzu. 'Me Dan.'

'Me Tom,' said McTruss.

Dinner was served à *chambre*.

'We have Preeking Druck,' said the Nip.

Ah, Peking Duck! The Inspector took a mouthful. Good God! It was like an old tyre. 'This duck is rubbery.'

'Oh, thank you werry much,' said Shitzu.

East is east and west is west etc., etc. The room phone rang. 'Hello?' Is the Inspector comfortable? 'Oh, yes.' Would the Inspector like a nightcap? No thanks, he always slept bareheaded.

Tired by a hard day's inspecting, McTruss fell into a deep sleep, he didn't see an old naked Jew wearing a capel and massaging a jelly pass through the room and exit out the back. Down the now dark corridor strode Lord O'Goldstein bending down to peer through keyholes and massage his jelly. Oh, how he missed London and the real thing . . . however, for now he'd have to be satisfied with the Aga Kuka's keyhole-shaped bum.

The sun was setting as Garda Sergeant Kelly drove along Drool lanes on his evening patrol. It was a pleasant drive, Clare County was beautiful in the summer, the rain was warmer. Through the soft rain mist in the setting sun he drove. Keep the speed steady, don't want to exceed the limit, only yesterday afternoon he had chased a car breaking the limit. It had been a tough chase on a bike, he had cautioned the driver, 'You've been doing fifty miles an hour.' The motorist had said, 'I haven't been out an hour!'

He steered his bike around a gentle curve. What was that directly ahead? Two fellas by a horse lying in the road, one bare-bummed man retrieving his trousers from under the horse. Kelly drew level. 'Is dat horse drunk?' he said, about to arrest it.

'No, der horse fainted,' said Rory.

'I'm not surprised with you dressed like that,' said Kelly.

'He'll be on his feet in a minute,' said Rory.

Not having feet, the animal tottered to its hooves.

Sergeant Kelly smelt the horse's breath, no sign of alcohol. 'He seems to be all right now,' said Kelly. 'Aren't you the Prune brothers?'

'No,' said Tige. '*I'm* not the Prune brothers, *we* are.'

114

Kelly cycled away none the wiser. He was a nice policeman as policeman go and as policemen go he went.

That was a near thing! Remounting the cart, the Prunes headed ever so slowly for home. Exhausted by the galloping, the animal let the brothers back it into a broken-down stable, this stallion who once ate selected bran, mashed, soaked in molasses and vitamin pills, ate his first turnips.

Several miles away Chief Inspector McTruss phoned Limerick Garda station and told them that the horse they were looking for was brown and possibly three-legged. At the same time Rory was dyeing the animal black. Alas, on the other side his brother was dyeing it white.

THE NIGHTMARE

With reservations Looney accepted the odd-job and jelly man with the naked lord. It was to be a trial week, a great trial, especially for Looney.

While the insensible Lord O'Goldstein lay unconscious on the couch, Looney helped Mrs Fitts to finish off the brandy. Then she said, 'He's still unconscious, just to be safe we better open another one!' After the third bottle she had put the gramophone on and danced the tango to 'La Paloma'.

On the way back, pissed to the point of perfidy, staggering back along the twilight road and sometimes forward, two kind men with a broken cart and a very slow horse gave Looney a lift. 'Jasus,' he had observed to them, 'isn't it – hic – time youse got rid o' – hic – dis donkey and got a new one.' The two men had laughed.

They dropped him off at the pub. By now the brandy had taken complete charge of his brain. 'Jasshus!' he said to the barman 'his, hi want sschome schome Ghyneiz.' The barman gave him one. Looney laid a pound on the counter then he ordered another 'Ghyneiz'. When he said he couldn't pay, the landlord gave him another one – it crashed on his chin like a brick on china.

When Looney came round he was lying face down on his back outside the pub. He rose to his feet and staggered singing into the night. It was three, four, five, six and seven o'clock as he tried to open the door. He tiptoed into the house with a CRASH! BANG! WALLOP! THUD! In a thrice *she* was there with folded arms and nostrils akimbo.

'What time do you call this?' she flamed.

'Oh darlin',' he drooled, 'did youse just stay up to ask me the time?'

'Fer God's sake, man!' she savaged. 'What did you get drunk for?'

'About a pound,' he said and crashed back on his bed in a drunken sleep.

What a nightmare of a dream! It was the High Court, there were his wife and son in mourning black! A Queen's Counsel was speaking: 'M'lud, the deceased Mick Looney of 113b Ethel Road, Kilburn, on the night in question after a bout of heavy night's drinking had repaired to the Camden and District Public Turkish Steam Baths. There he disrobed. He was conducted to a cubicle by an attendant who then turned on the steam. Alas, owing to a faulty valve, the temperature in Mr Looney's cubicle rose to two hundred and eighty degrees Fahrenheit! The melting point of the human body.' Mrs Looney let off a terrible sob. The QC continued, 'Within twenty minutes Mr Looney had melted and lay in a steaming pool on the floor!'

Looney groaned and turned in his bed.

'Fortunately,' the QC went on, 'an alert attendant rushed to Mr Looney and with a sponge mopped him up and squeezed him into a bucket.'

There was his dear wife sobbing, no! Those weren't sobs, she was *laughing*!

'Order in court,' rapped the judge. 'In a bucket, you say?'

'In a bucket, I say,' retorted the QC.

'Is the plaintiff in court?' asked the judge.

'Yes, m'lud, he's in that bucket.' The QC pointed to Exhibit No. 1.

In his drunken sleep Looney started to sweat with fear. The dream continued relentlessly.

'Can we see the plaintiff's present condition?' said the judge.

The QC instructed the Clerk of the Court, 'Pour out Mr Looney.' Slowly the clerk emptied Looney out into a tall glass specimen jar.

In his sleep Looney groaned out loud. 'Shut up, yer bastard,' shouted Mrs Looney from her bed.

From her place in court, however, she was trying to stifle hysterical laughter with a handkerchief.

117

'Three pints and four fluid ounces,' said the Clerk of the Court removing a dipstick.

'I see,' said the judge, 'I presume the Looney family are suing Camden Council for negligence?'

The QC shook his head. 'No, m'lud, they are suing for short measure! You see, the correct measure for a man of Mr Looney's size is two and a half gallons . . .'

The dream was fading as Looney tossed in his bed, it was changing in a swirling cloud. For a moment there was a barmaid with big tits from Kilburn, but now, no, it was the graveside, there were his dear wife and son dressed in black. What's this? Four men carrying a coffin-sized Guinness bottle, him inside it! They are pouring it into the grave! The priest laughing and intoning, 'We commit to the earth the mortal remains of Mick Looney . . .'

With a terrible scream Looney awoke.

'What in God's name is it, man?' said his wife.

'Ohhhhhhhhh,' gasped Looney, 'I've had a terrible terrible dream.' He flopped back on his bed. Never again, he said, never, never, never, nevezer . . . nevezzzer . . . nevezzzzzzz.

THE SHEEPDOG TRIAL

It was one of those days, that's how they come in Ireland, in ones, in ones, in those, in days, yes, it was one of those one days when you could smell fried eggs, it was that kind of day for Charlie McCafferty, he was up before the lark. Normally he was up before the magistrate, the usual, drunk, drunk in charge, drunk in charge of a donkey, drunk under a donkey, sober in charge of a drunk donkey, and, he could smell fried eggs, the magistrate had cautioned him, 'You must give it up,' he said. 'Jasus, I have,' said McCafferty, 'you should ha' seen me when I was really on it.' and fried eggs.

Yes, it was one of those days. He arose at five-thirty in time to turn the alarm off before it woke him up, he leapt from his bed, opened the window, took a deep breath, ah! he could smell fried eggs. Raising his skinny arms heavenwards, revealing hairy armpits like relatives of the nudist woman with a fanny like a deserted crow's nest, plunging down, he touched his toes, ah! fried eggs! Next, like Dr Jekyll, he started to change for the big day. Today was the Drool and District Sheepdog Trials. Now, should he wear this tie? Or that tie? He put on a that tie.

In the kitchen his aged one-legged mother Silé hopped around preparing his breakfast, flavoured by ash from her cigarette. Having one leg had its drawbacks, she had to advertise, 'One-legged woman wishes to meet one right-legged woman with a view to buying a pair of shoes.' Silé hopped and hummed a DIY tune, it was to music what Colonel Gadaffi was to medieval brass rubbing.

Like the instructions from a Portolano, the aroma of cooking sailed up the stairs over a sleeping pussycat and finally assaulted the nostrils of McCafferty, sending the

119

gastric juices whirlygigging in his swonnicles. 'Ah! fried eggs,' he said. Putting a rosary in his waistcoat and a crucifix in his rear trousers pocket (he liked God's protection fore and aft) he sauntered down the stairs. 'By Gor, Mudder, dem fried eggs smell lovely.' He seated himself at the plain wooden table and read the plain wooden *Dublin Times*.

'I see der vote has gone against divorce,' he said. 'Oh yes,' hopped Silé. 'It's no good, they'll have ter make adultery legal.'

Hopping, his mother transported the sizzling frying pan of bacon and cabbage to the table. He took a mothful then stopped, really he wanted to take a mouthful. 'Dis isn't fried eggs,' he said.

This, dear reader, was his trouble, he could *only* smell fried eggs, be it ham, turkey, onions, fish, liver, he'd smell fried eggs. The night the hayricks had caught fire he sat up in bed and said, 'I smell fried eggs.' His wife had put on Allure, an expensive perfume. 'Like it?' she said. 'Fried eggs,' said he.

The doctor said there was no cure. 'You've got naso-ovum-oderatus syndrome.'

'Oh?' said McCafferty. 'What would that be?'

'That would be five pounds,' said the doctor. 'There's only one cure, have fried eggs every day.'

'I demand a second opinion,' said McCafferty.

The doctor gave it and that was another five pounds. 'I smell fried eggs,' he said.

The Drool Sheepdog Trials; the day was clear and sunny as they all assembled in Maughan Field. The whole district was out to lay bets, or wimmin. There were three entrants, One, Two and Three; McCafferty, Pat Moloney and Len Byrne.

The two judges were under the oak tree with score cards, poteen and binoculars, farmers all. If they dropped the atom bomb here now it would wipe out Irish agriculture in the west and the world would be none the wiser. ATOM BOMB DROPPED ON DROOL, NO DAMAGE AT ALL would be the headline.

The Scottish black-faced sheep stood protestant-like mid-field in an unsuspecting flock, the first contestant! Charlie McCafferty and his dog Boy, he originally named it Bernard in

120

honour of Shaw, but considering it old-fashioned he named it John after Lennon. Such was his admiration for the Beatles that after a month he called the puzzled dog after McCartney, a month later George, next Ringo, finally Boy after Boy George, a great honour in Drool. The dog was so paranoid he would answer to *any* name. Now Bernard-John-Paul-George-and-Boy sat on his bum in the wet grass looking up at his master wondering what name he was today.

The judges rang a bell, the great Drool Sheepdog Trial was on! At a whistled command, Boy set off in a long looping run to get behind the flock. Apart from the smell of fried eggs, so far so good, the air was filled with the high fluctuating whistles of McCafferty as the dog zig-zagged behind the flock. I'm doin' powerful well, thought McCafferty, but all good things come to an end. Among the starling flocks of Drool was a particularly intelligent one, shall we call him Puck? Puck was a superb mimic: first he mastered the sound of the trim-phone that had people running to answer it; for a while now all around the district he had picked up the various shepherds' whistles and was fluent in all of them. It was a moment when McCafferty was on the verge of getting the sheep in the pen that Puck took a hand. Suddenly, unexplainably, Boy drove the sheep in a series of circles, took them off in a northern direction, made them swim a stream, tried to drive them up a tree and despite McCafferty's apoplectic whistles disappeared with them over Maughan Hill.

Drool was stunned. McCafferty sussed it out first. 'It's a fockin' starlin'!' he said, running to his van for his shotgun. The assembled multitude were then treated to McCafferty hurtling across field after field firing at any bird he saw. An innocent crow got it in the arse. 'Caw-blimey,' it croaked. At once the bookies started to call odds on his chances of success – for a while he was 7 to 2 on. The bangs and swearing from McCafferty continued as he gradually became a speck in the distance. Disappointed, the crowd started to drift away. Only a few aficionados remained with the odds sliding to 40 to 1. Finally he stumbled back, a 100-to-1, mud-splattered, broken man.

121

'Here,' said Len Byrne at 5 to 1, 'let me try.' He grabbed the barrel and screaming dropped it and his odds to 20 to 1. 'Ohhhhh me hands,' he wailed, placing a burnt member under an armpit, jack-knifing up and down moaning.

'God, you'd think he'd become a Mohammdan,' said someone.

'Oh, it's bloody hot,' wailed Byrne.

The crowd, up to then bored, perked up as new betting went on to McCafferty who was going to try again. With the smell of fried eggs, he started to search every tree and bush. Blazing away, he could hear 'dat bloody starlin'' whistling in the middle of a flock of starlings which he started to chase across the countryside; firing into a bush, he peppered the legs of a pair of lovebirds. The injured lover, a six foot giant clutched his area and chased McCafferty at 100 to 1 almost out of the county. Even there he could smell fried eggs.

THE CRACK

The talk of the district was the robbery of Sherbert. Was he three-legged or down to two? In the pub it was the main topic. Looney sat at a table sipping the night-black Guinness into his tubular interior.

'Is anybody sitting here?' said village idiot Jasper McQuonk, pointing to an empty seat.

'Fer God's sake, man,' said Looney, 'you can *see* there's nobody sittin' dere.'

'Oh yes,' said Jasper, 'I could see dere was nobody sittin' dere, but I thought I would get a second opinion.'

With that, the two men looked at each other, it was a moment in time, and that's about all.

Holding his drink with both hands, Jasper slowly sat down and with both hands smiled at Looney. 'Slawnchegewa,' he said, and with both hands sipped another decimal profit into the Guinness family coffers. Were it known, Ireland was a land of liquid shareholders, the only dividend was getting pissed. 'Did youse hear about dat horse bein' stoled?' said Jasper with both hands. Looney nodded.

The wonders of the human body are endless. Approaching was Terence Joyce, sixty-two, flowing white hair, a white beard and a pound of dandruff to match – Joyce, ex-Abbey actor and a postal correspondence philosopher. 'Pray, is anybody sitting here?' he said with a sweeping bow.

'No,' said Looney politely.

He's changed his attitude, thought Jasper.

'Ahhhhhh,' said Terence Joyce sitting down flamboyantly, then with a wave said, 'Life, gentlemen, is a series of unexpected unexplained incidents that come and go like sudden storms.'

123

'Yes,' said Jasper, who thought it was a weather report, 'yes, I tink we'll have more rain tonight.'

Joyce bit his lip.

'Did youse hear about dat horse being stoled?' said Jasper with both hands.

Terence Joyce smiled and nodded. He hadn't a clue what the boy was on about (actually he was on about a pound a week). 'Ah, the horse,' said Joyce.

'He means der one dat was stolen from der Aga Kuka,' said Looney.

Joyce smiled anew, he hadn't a clue what Looney was talking about either. 'Ah, the Aga Kuka,' he said, 'ah yessss.' He nodded, shaking free three ounces of dandruff. 'Yes, the horse *and* the Aga Kuka . . .' With a penetrating look in his eyes, he gave a faraway stare into some mystic timeless repository of space. 'There's an oldddd Irish saying,' he said. Looney and Jasper craned forward. Joyce lingered a moment and then said, 'I can't quite think of it at the moment.'

Jasper gave a wide appreciative grin. 'Oh dat's clever,' he said and slowly repeated it. 'There's an oldddd Irish sayin' . . . Oh yes, dat's clever, I'll remember dat.'

There had not been such an ill-matched trio since Hitler, Mussolini and Tojo. They were interrupted by Shamus Looney, still reeking of dung from his day's muck-spreading, he brought his own flies with him. 'Evenin' all,' he said setting down on the bench. He set his glass to his lips, in one long gulp the contents disappeared from sight to reappear, unfortunately for him, at 5 a.m. the following morning. 'Ah,' he said from his froth-ridden lips, 'dat's better.'

That isn't better, thought Jasper and said, 'I tink it's better when der glass is full, ha ha.'

'Ahhh! A full glass,' enunciated Joyce, 'a full glass is like a midnight rose.'

They all thought about that quite a bit.

'And, er, why is a full glass like der midnight rose, mister?' said Looney.

Joyce turned his head and faced him. 'Why,' he said, 'ha ha ha, because, my dear fellow, it is written.'

124

This wasn't good enough, thought Looney. 'Written? Where?'

Again Looney was treated to Joyce's smiling, knowing, slightly contemptuous glance. 'In the book.'

'Der book?' queried Looney. 'What bloody book?'

Joyce sucked in air and breathed out with a look of despair. 'If only we knew,' he said.

Looney wasn't going to be outdone. 'Der thylacine is extinct in Tasmania,' he said.

Jasper McQuonk turned to Shamus. 'Dere's an old Irish sayin',' he said, grinning knowingly. 'How did you like dat?' he said triumphantly.

Like all Irish bars, so continued the multi-conversations. Der hatom bomb is der ting that dominates der world – oh yes, but the power of faith is greater, ah yes, bombs will come and bombs will go but a lot of people will go wid dem, faith won't bloody stop dat, mister – ah yes, dat's der will of God – I didn't know he left a will – will you hark at him, der Russians don't believe in God – so? So dey got der bloody bomb – Nilgiri Hills, tea-growing area in western India – Der Vatican haven't got der bomb – Dey got der Pope – ah well, they can't afford both – Five times a night! – Wot good's der Pope if dey drops der bomb on the Vatican – Dey'll have annuder Pope, dat'll teach 'em – Five times a night? – I want to die a natural death, like being mugged – America will save us – It didn't save Glen Miller – It didn't even save Max Miller – I tell you, Black Devil will piss the Curragh dis year – I don't tink dey'll drop der bomb on Ireland – Why not? Who der fock in dere right mind would bomb Ireland? – Ian Paisley – Dere's a looney – Dey said der CIA killed Glen Miller – Der Hanging Gardens of Babylon 3000 BC – Der CIA killed Kennedy fer fuckin' Marilyn Monroe – Black Devil? Don't make me laff – Five times a night – Dis Guinness is as thin as bloody water – Day say Glen Miller is still alive livin' in Mongolia – I smell fried eggs – She picks dem up in the street – Who does? – Mudder Theresa – Picks up what? – Wogs – She's wastin' her time, as fast as you pick one up annuder twenty thousand fall down – Frankie Howerd was on

125

der same plane – No, dat was Leslie Howard – Dere's a difference? – Yes, one's alive and one's dead – Dat's a big difference – He fucked Marilyn Monroe? – It's der bottled stuff, dat's why – Meat gives you cancer – Five times a night, eh? – The giant squid is sixty feet long – AIDS will come to Ireland – No, we don't have enough homosexuals – Der Pope is 6 to 1 fer the Curragh if dey don't bomb Ireland fer fucking Marilyn Monroe in the Nilgiri Hills picking up wogs in the streets of Mongolia with Frankie Howerd mugged to a natural death by Sister Theresa with homosexual AIDS.

Yes, the Sherbert robbery was the talk of the pub. Did it have three or was it down to one leg? At the bar Sergeant Kelly spoke in a hushed whisper with Inspector McTruss.

'They're not so easy to get,' said McTruss, 'but when I can get them, I prefer Bassets' Liquorice Allsorts.'

'Is that a fact?' whispered Kelly. 'Meself, I like Bluebird Toffees.'

'Here you are, gentlemen,' said barman Riddick, putting down two glasses of Jamesons. 'That'll be two pounds.'

Kelly drove his hand into his pocket. 'No no no,' insisted McTruss. 'Let me.' So Kelly let him. 'The Aga is putting up a reward for any information about Sherbert.'

'A reward? How much?' said Kelly.

'A thousand pounds,' said McTruss.

A man could do a lot with a thousand pounds, like spend it, thought Kelly. 'Has anybody come forward?'

McTruss nodded, he pointed towards Jasper. 'Him.'

'Oh,' said Kelly, 'what did he say?'

McTruss smirked. 'Nothing, he just came forward.'

Like the vandalised public toilet, there wasn't much to go on. McTruss cast an eye around the pub, the criminal could actually be here in this very room! At this moment! If not, somewhere in Drool, or County Clare or in Ireland . . . He might also be in Ulster, England, Scotland or Wales, perhaps the Continent! Or in America, in fact he might be anywhere!

'We got the Whole Drool force on the lookout,' said Kelly. 'In fact, he's out at this moment.'

THE PHANTOM SINGER II

Indeed Garda O'Brien was, in his full midnight vocal phantom costume. After his last singing raid on the Gronnivans the write-up in the *Drool Bugle* hadn't been that good. He had the cuttings.

PHantoM SINGer SCHICK HORROr

Drool. Wnesday EEarly on the mornig of last nighT, Mr and Mrs GronniVan @ ⅔, were held up by a £ masked intruder in their bed rOOm, the IIntruder was describeD by Mr Gronnivan as seven foot and 900 inches, and by Mrs Gronnivan as five feet six possibly 'a nig- ger', at gun point HE £2 forced themm to listen to him sing ½ obscene songs like Ramona and Rise Marie.

O'Brien was outraged, he had not sung either of those songs! What a terrible review for his first night! Very well, next time he would choose someone with class.

He had looked up the phone book and found an ex-directory man who would know about music. That is why at two in the morning Lord O'Goldstein and his jelly were sitting up in bed cowering before the shotgun of the hooded singer who was saying, 'You'll clap, you bastard, understand.'

Lord O'Goldstein nodded, anything rather than money. 'Is it a robbery?' he said.

'No, no,' said the phantom.

'Is it a kidnapping?'

'No, no.'

For a moment Lord O'Goldstein's heart beat a little faster. 'Are you a pervert?' he said hopefully.

'No,' said the phantom. As he spoke, a hooded banjo player climbed through the window, oh yes, O'Brien had gone up market, he had bribed Lonnie Donovan the Drool banjoist to accompany him, a pound for the night.

For a terrible baffling hour, when he should have been playing with his red jelly, Lord O'Goldstein was subjected to the quivering nasal tenor singing the whole score of *The Student Prince*. For dear life O'Goldstein applauded, squashing his jelly.

'Shout encore, you bastard,' said the phantom.

'Look,' objected O'Goldstein, 'I'm an old man.'

'OK, say it slower,' said O'Brien.

'Listen,' said the old pervert, 'if you sing through the keyhole of that door I'll pay you fifty pounds.'

Phantom was halted in his tracks. After paying the banjo player his pound that would leave, that would leave, why, forty-seven! Keeping O'Goldstein and his squashed jelly at gunpoint, the phantom and his banjo player retreated behind the door while O'Goldstein reached out to his bedside fridge and took out a fresh jelly. O'Brien knelt down and placed his mouth to the keyhole and sang, 'Be my love', then rushed into the room and shouted, 'Clap, you bastard, and where's the money?'

'Will you take a cheque?' said the lord.

'Only if you've got a bank card.'

The phantom banjo player intervened. 'I want mine in cash,' he insisted.

Lord O'Goldstein lifted up the mattress and took out a handful of pounds from the two million in cash he kept there. He always made his own bed, that's why he would lie in it, he even lied to the phantom. 'That's all I got,' he said, giving him thirty-six pounds. 'You said fifty,' said the phantom.

'Yes, I said fifty,' said O'Goldstein, 'but since then times have been bad.'

'O'Brien had to admit that times had been bad. For a start he was eight pounds short of the fifty he'd been promised. Singing 'Come, come, I love you only', he backed out of the window. No accidents this time, his banjo player securely holding the bottom of the ladder waiting with his banjo, with which he laid out O'Brien robbing him of the thirty-six pounds.

THE POST OFFICE ROBBERY

Upstairs at Drool Farm the Prune brothers' ageing father Dermot fossicked around the room looking for the long underpants he was wearing. Dermot was very old, eighty-nine, very very tall, six foot six. These days he walked with a slight stoop, which made him five foot seven. He opened the drawers of the chest of drawers .... 'Ahhhhhhhhhhhhhhhhhh,' he said .... no, not this one, he opened the one below, 'Ahhhhhhhhhhhhhhhhhhhh,' he said .... 'Oh dear' .... 'Oh' .... 'Tsu, tsu' .... 'Tsu, tsu' ...... 'No, not in there, the one below?' .... 'Oh dear' .... 'Dear, oh dear, oh dear' .... 'Ahhh' .... 'Has anybody seen?' .... 'I wonder how Molly is' .... 'Ohhh, locked' .... 'Now where can they be?' .... 'See' .... 'Has anybody seen?' .... 'Would you look at that?' .... 'Ahhhhhhhhhhhhhhhhhhhh' ....

Downstairs, his two sons were adding up the damage.

Estimate for repairing two wrecked stalls...	£10.00
Repair of peat cart	£ 5.00
Horse feed	£ 7.00
New trousers	£ 1.50

'Dis horse is a bloody distaster!' said Rory. '*Twenty-two pounds!*' The Prune brothers had a cash-flow problem.

'How much is twenty-two pounds?' said Tige.

129

'Ohhh, it's a lot.'

'Yes, but is it a *lot* lot or a *little* lot?'

'It's a *lot-lot*, a *bloody lot-lot*.'

Where are they going to get that much money? The first practical thing to do was empty that bottle of poteen. When they had drained it, they were no nearer the twenty-two pounds, but an inspired plot came to Rory. Through narrowed eyes he said, 'Give me dat walking stick' – difficult to say through narrowed eyes.

Drool Post Office was very very busy, twelve pensions today! All morning with a concerto of arthritic hands clutching treasured pension books they stood in an obedient queue. At the desk Post Mistress Jolly paid out fragile amounts to even more fragile clients with the indifference of an animal vivisector. Her command of 'Next!' rang out like a Gestapo Kapo at the door of a gas chamber. Now the queue was down to the last victim, Rose Bridie, somewhere between seventy and eighty, a virgin from birth, the nearest she got to sex was feeling a jam roll or eating a Mars bar in bed.

The now desperate Prune brothers had timed it well. With an embarrassed clumping walk, they got in the queue. Finally Miss Bridie tottered away to buy yet another jam roll and Mars bar. The Prunes came forward.

'Ahhh, Rory,' said Miss Jolly with a smile that broke her face. She fancied Rory, he was like a young Greek dog, short, with the physique of a hat stand; bad eyesight had its rewards.

'Good mornin', Miss Jolly,' said Rory. Pulling down a mask, he raised his walking stick in a threatening manner. 'Dis is a stick-up.'

Miss Jolly smiled. 'Yes, I can see your stick is up,' she said suggestively and burst out laughing.

Was this woman mad? Didn't she know her life was in danger, hadn't she ever seen *Police Five*? 'Stop dat laughin',' he warned. 'Dis is a robbery and a very *serious* one.'

'Robbery,' she said, then robbery she thought. Quickly she put up the sign 'Position Closed'.

'Dat don't frighten us,' said Tige over Rory's shoulder.

'Shut up,' said Rory.

'Look, boys,' she said. 'Are you both out of your minds? What will the neighbours say?'

Fuck the neighbours, thought the Prunes, which in fact they had already done. 'Don't try anything funny,' said Tige over Rory's shoulder.

Miss Jolly frowned. Why in God's name at a time like this did they think she was was going to do something funny? 'Have you been drinking?' she said.

'No.'

'Well, have, have you been *eating*, then?'

It was getting silly, this woman was *ruining* a carefully planned robbery.

'In any case, this Post Office can't afford a robbery,' she said. 'Why don't you try a big city like Limerick?'

The Prune brothers did an identical pause. 'Lie on the floor,' said Rory. 'Like they do on television,' he added.

Complainingly she lay down. 'You wait until I see your mother,' she said.

They weren't going to wait till she saw their mother, in any case she was dead. 'Now we want,' Rory paused and referred to a piece of paper, 'twenty-two pounds. If you don't, we'll smash dis inkwell.'

'I can't reach the money from here, you idiots,' she said to the floor.

'Stand up,' threatened Rory.

Alas, at that moment Mr Timothy Dicker, the Post Master, ushered from his office in great distress; the batteries on his hearing aid, like his wife's tits, were flat. 'What are you lying on the floor for, Miss Jolly?' he said.

'It's a robbery,' said Miss Jolly. 'Like you see on television,' she added.

Mr Dicker looked at his watch. 'It's twenty past eleven,' he said.

Rory could see the money in the cashbox, it was now or never, he settled for now. Dropping his stick, he made to leap the counter, caught his boots on the lip and fell head first on the other side breaking his leg and ending up on top of Miss Jolly.

'Darling,' she said as he writhed in agony. 'Not here,' she added.

The ambulance arrived and took Rory, his broken leg and his stick away.

'Next,' said Miss Jolly.

THE CHILDREN

The Prunes, in desperation, had let the great stallion Sherbert go. They put him in a field facing away from them and whacked him on the rump, away ran a thousand pounds' reward. Eithne Molloy and her brother Michael put down their picnic basket, then sat by a dreaming childstream throwing pebbles, an important thing to do when you're six and seven. Hearing a noise behind them, they turned to see a black and white horse.

'Look at that!' said Michael in child wonder.

'He's black *and* whited,' said Eithne. 'He must be magic.'

Pulling handfuls of grass and, being farm children, without fear, they fed the great horse. This horse was bigger than their farm one.

'Look at his longed legs,' said Michael.

'Yes,' said Eithne, 'that's 'cos he's a long long long long way up.'

The two children circumnavigated the great horse.

'He goes orl the way round,' said Eithne.

'Yes,' said Michael, 'an' he goes up and over too, I like the black side.'

'I'll have the white side,' said Eithne. 'Girls should always have white 'cos they're smaller.'

'I'm going to give him some pickernick,' said Michael, unwrapping a packet.

Soon the great million-pound stallion was munching his first cheese sandwich. Eithne was not long in introducing him to the mysteries of the banana.

'Oh he like-ed that,' she said, feeding it to him skin and all.

Michael laughed. 'You didn't take the skin off.'

133

'No,' said Eithne. 'That way he getted more.' Girls are much more sensible than boys. 'I'm going to patted *my* side,' said Eithne, stroking the great chest of the horse. 'I wonder where he sleeped,' she said.

'Shall we take him back home?' said Michael.

'No, no,' said Miss Eithne, girls are much more sensible than boys, 'no, he's magic, we got to keep him secret.'

'Let's take him for a niceee walk,' said Michael, taking the halter rope.

'I must hol-ed the rope, too,' said Miss Eithne. 'He's half of mine.'

Together they led the great horse around the hedgerowed field, the summer sun blazed as they walked through daisy-punctuated grass. The children stopped to blow dandelion parachutes on to the August wind. A cabbage white alighted on the horse's flank and rode on him until rested, then took to its appointment with the summer, its zig-zag flight like a counterpoint to the wind.

'What shall we call him,' said the boy.

The girl put a finger in her mouth. 'I'm going to call my side Ariel like Mummy's wash powder.'

'I'll call my side Jim,' he said.

'I wish I could reached up and ride on him,' she said, holding the horse's leg.

Michael looked up at the great horse, his back seemed so far away. 'He's nearly upped to the sky,' he said.

'I know! Tomorrow let's bringed a ladder,' said Eithne as, girls being much more sensible than boys, leading Jim-Ariel back to their basket, they laid out their picnic.

The great horse quietly grazed as the children ate sand-wiches, fairy cakes and lemonade. Two currant buns made the million-pound horse their friend for life.

THE FAYRE

As I watched her wander
O'er the heath
Black was the colour
Of my true love's teeth.
As I watched him wander
Through the fayre
Bald was the colour of my true love's hair.

Old Irish Love Song

Mick Looney, heir apparent or apparent heir, and his apparent wife wandered through the Drool Fayre gradually becoming a repository for candy floss, sodium-salted peanuts, Watney's Pale, sodium-salted crisps, ice-cream, Watney's Pale, cheese and ham sandwiches, Polo mints, milkshakes, chocolate, Watney's Pale, scotch eggs, all accompanied by the steam organ in the carousel. As its music percolated across the greenacious fields, the roundabout carried timelost children on revolving wooden-horsed dreams; wide-eyed, the children looked on to some timeless horizon known only to children and butterflies.

Maureen O'Higgins, six summers old, sucked her pink candy floss, she was a princess on a white horse riding the clouds until she found her wings:

Round and around went the girl on the roundabout
Lost in a world no one's foundabout.

Little Terence Donovan was riding a yellow-spotted charger, galloping towards the enemy:

135

Candy floss, a painted horse, a chocolate cream,
The ingredients you need to make a dream.

'Ah ha!' said Looney, stopping outside a badly erected ex-army tent held down with clothes' pegs clipped to the grass. 'See dat?' he said, and pointed to an ill-written sign on a piece of cardboard. 'ALI MUSTAPHER – ANCIENT EGYP-TIAN KLAIRVOYANT AND TOBACCONIST.'

What luck! Here was one of those fellas that could tell the future. He explained to his queen, 'He makes a pot of tea, den he pours it into a mug.'

The queen was unimpressed, why did she marry him! 'Den,' went on the heir apparent, 'den he pours der tea into der mug, den guess what?'

'He drinks it,' said Mrs Looney.

'No no no,' said he. 'No, he pours all der tea out just leavin' der leaves.'

Why did she marry him?

'Den he *looks* at der leaves!'

Why, why why did she marry him? Mind you, she had met him when her glasses were at the menders, during which time he proposed and she accepted. He told her he was 'catering for a large company', catering? He was a bloody tea boy on a building site!

Back to reality, he was still going on, 'Den he *reads* der tea leaves.' He gave a wink, nod and tapped his nose.

Why did she marry him?

Childlike, he ran his finger across the writing. 'Fifty pee a seshun, I'm having' a shot. Dis feller might be able to tell if I'm descended from der Kings.'

As Looney entered the tent, Ian Shaunnessy, a dustman from Limerick, adjusted a turban made from knotted socks. 'What do youse want, O wise one?' he said, touching his forehead like he'd seen on the tellyvision.

Wise one? thought Looney. Dis is a good start.

The interior of the tent was purposely dark, it made it hard to see that Shaunnessy was wearing a poncho made from an army blanket with a hole in the middle. 'Do youse want fags or der predictions?' he said, indicating an inverted tea chest laid out with cigarettes.

'I'll have der predictions,' said Looney, sitting on a very low milking stool bringing his head just above the level of the table.

'Now,' said the klairvoyant. He gobbed through the tent flap and started to stroke and stare into a small glass ball that until yesterday was a paperweight at the Post Office. Wiping his nose on the back of his sleeve he said, 'Ahhhhhhhhhhhhhhhhhh-hh,' then silence.

Looney broke it. 'Now what?' he said.

'Now,' said the klairvoyant. 'Fifty pee.'

Looney balked. 'But youse haven't dun anything yet,' he said.

Actually he had, but so far it hadn't reached Looney's side. ''Tis written,' he chanted in a thick Irish accent. 'Der seer of Cairo and District cannot work until der palm has been crossed wid der silver or der fifty pee.'

Looney felt in his trilby hatband and drew out the coin and placed it in the klairvoyant's hand. 'Is dat right youse can tell der future?'

The wise man nodded. 'Only fer a certain distance,' he said.

'Fer instance?'

'Fer instance, tomorrow.' He closed his eyes and looked up. 'Tomorrow is Sunday.'

'I know dat,' said Looney.

'Ah! *Now* you do,' said the seer.

'I mean, can youse tell me what's goin ter *happen* tomorrow?' said the heir apparent.

'Yes,' said the seer. 'Tomorrow, first Mass will be six-tirty, den nine o'clock, High Mass at twelve, rain in places, but clearing up later.'

Looney frowned. This was highly suspicious. 'Is dat as far as you can tell?'

The seer nodded and sneezed, splattering Looney and the glass ball with a mist of spittle. 'Yer see,' went on the wise Limerick dustman, 'I'm a klairvoyant and tobacconist wid a difference. I can tell der past, fer instance.' He looked closely

137

into the spittle-covered glass ball. 'Red Rum won der English Grand National.'

Looney sat bolt upright, by Gor he was right! Red Rum *did* win the National. 'Any more like dat?' he said eagerly.

'Oh yes,' said the seer. He closed his eyes and grabbed his forehead with his hand, missed but got it a second time. 'I see it comin' through, yes, in nineteen tirty-nine England declared war on der Germans.'

The man was right again, this was amazing! Perhaps! . . . Looney leaned forward making the edge of the table press his adam's apple. In a strange castrated voice he said, 'Can youse go back to der Kings of Ireland?'

'Dat means annuder fifty pee.'

What luck! thought Looney, for fifty pee he might be a king, then he could get a second mortgage. Taking his trilby hat off, he felt inside the hatband and came out with a coin and half the lining. The seer inspected it, then placed it in his pocket.

Unannounced a very fat woman entered the tent. She wore a long black dress, boots and a spotted handkerchief around her head gypsy-style, and reeking of bacon. 'Sorry it's late,' she said through a wracking bronchial cough, 'but I been readin' a lot of dese silly buggers' palms.' She set down a chipped enamel mug of steaming tea and a cheese sandwich, then coughed her way out of the tent.

'Dat's Fatima, me wife,' said the seer biting into the sandwich.

'Dat's a bad cough she's got,' said Looney.

'Oh yes, you don't get many good ones round here,' said the seer. With a mouthful he continued, 'Now how far back?' he said.

Looney paused. 'Well, till you reach a king called Looney.'

The seer sipped the tea. 'OK, ohhhhhhhhh,' he moaned, still munching. 'I see,' munch, munch, 'far far backkkkkkkkk,' much, munch, swallow, bite, 'ohh yes, dere's lots of,' munch, munch, 'kings, ahhhhh, I can't go back any furder.'

'Why not?' said Looney.

'I've run out of fifty pees.'

Looney passed another coin.

'Ah yes! I can see a high king, and his name is, his name is, what's *yer* name?' said the seer.

'Looney.'

'What a coincidence! Dis one's called Looney as well.'

A great smile came over Looney's unshaven face. 'Listen,' he said excitedly, 'would youse write dat down and sign it?'

Shaunnessy tore the back off a cigarette packet and wrote down the information and signed it. He was yet another man called X.

Holding the precious document, Looney ushered forth into the sunlight. To a baffled wife he held up the back of the fag packet. 'Read dat.'

She did, aloud: 'Sweet Afton Ireland's own cigarette.'

Snatching it from her (it tore leaving half in her hand), snatching her bit, he pieced them together and read: 'This man is King Afton, Ireland's Looney cigarette. Ah fuck,' he said rearranging the pieces.

'What are youse on about?' she said.

'Never mind, I'll tell you later.' Carefully he placed the two pieces in his jacket pocket, carefully dropping both on the ground.

THE PHANTOM UNMASKED

Young, fresh-faced, eager, not long from Dublin Police College, Novice Garda Neil Lynch now attached to the Drool Garda did his first morning patrol. Along a lonely mist-morned back street, he heard Gaelic groans. They led him to the semi-conscious figure of the phantom singer. Here before his very eyes was his first mysterious mystery. What category was this? a) a freshly unmurdered body; b) heavily disguised in evening dress; c) a shattered banjo. It was a Raffles-type situation with musical suspicions. Lynch pulled off the hood. Mother o' God, 'twas Garda O'Brien himself.

'Oh, it's my head,' groaned O'Brien. He was right, it was his. How terrible being laid out with a banjo; still, it was more romantic than a crowbar. He had some explaining to do, so he dooed it.

Lynch took the whole amazing tale down. O'Brien was in fact a secret nocturnal window cleaner. People who went to sleep with dirty windows woke up with them sparkling clean. But why the full evening dress? Ah, that was to bring a touch of romance to an otherwise mundane job. And the IRA-style hood? Mystery, and if his clients awoke during his nocturnal foray they would not be able to identify him; he was modest, he sought no fame. But the shattered banjo, that was his downfall. A felon had awaited him, felled him with the instrument and departed with O'Brien's wallet.

Taking it all down, Lynch called the ambulance. It took O'Brien to the Drool Cottage Hospital, the world's greatest medical disaster. The one doctor was seventy-eight and only yesterday had heard of penicillin – mind you penicillin never made much noise. O'Brien lay in bed awaiting suture. They were wheeling in a new patient. Two straining attendants

140

rolled the newcomer on to the next bed; the man held his leg and groaned.

'What's the trouble?' said O'Brien.

The man groaned again. 'I tink I've fractured me leg,' he said.

O'Brien commiserated. Would he like a song to cheer him up? No thanks. How did he break it? The man rolled over on one side.

'Can youse keep a secret?' said the man.

'For up to seven hours,' said O'Brien.

'Well, I did it tryin' ter rob der Post Office,' said Prune.

O'Brien stiffened in his bed. What incredible luck! Right here in the hospital he'd caught a bank robber. In a new strange official voice, he said, 'What is your name?'

The man rolled on his side again. 'Rory Prune, what's yours?'

Still in the supine concussed position, he said, 'O'Brien, I am a member of the Garda.'

Undaunted, Prune held out his hand. 'Oh, I pleased ter meet yer.'

O'Brien shook the hand. 'Rory Prune,' he cautioned, 'I'm arresting you . . .' He got no further, as they took Prune away to plaster his leg. O'Brien watched him go, he'd get him on the way back.

Mild, muttering, aged nurse Mildred O'Shea carried her tray of pills. 'Here's your painkiller,' she said, erroneously giving O'Brien a heavy-duty sleeping pill. When Prune returned, O'Brien was in a deep Tuinal sleep.

At midnight O'Brien woozed awake. Duty calls. 'Rory Prune,' he said, 'I arrest you for the Drool Post Office robbery. I warn you that anything you say will be taken down and used in evidence,' he said to the sleeping Prune. Never mind – YAWN – he'd get him – YAWN – tomorrow morning.

Awake for morning in a bowl of light . . . O'Brien awoke in a bowl of light, ah, there was Prune eating breakfast. 'Rory Prune,' he said, 'I arrest you . . .' He got no further as he was whisked away for suture. Never mind, he'd get him on the way back.

In suture they shaved the back of his head making him look as though his face was re-emerging behind him with his eyes and nose to follow. 'Oh dear,' said the aged surgeon, 'you need twelve stitches, we only go up to five. They'll have to send you to Limerick to get the other seven.'

His head covered with sticking plaster, O'Brien was wheeled back. Now the cop: 'Rory Prune, I . . .' But Prune was in a deep sleep under a 'painkiller'. Never mind he'd get him when he came to.

There was no escape. O'Brien awoke at six o'clock. Prune was awake too because they had taken him away to plaster his leg, having done the wrong one. OK, he'd get him when he came back! Sure enough, here came Prune back with his other leg in plaster. let him get settled, then strike. Prune smiled at O'Brien. Now, strike! 'Rory Prune. . . .' But no, they wheeled O'Brien away for X-rays. Never mind he'd get him when he came back.

When O'Brien returned they had screens around Prunes' bed. Got him! He's on the pan! He's trapped! In the whole history of crime no man had ever escaped from a bedpan. O'Brien stood close to the screens, he could hear straining. 'I arrest you for the Drool Post Office robbery. Anything you say will be taken down in evidence and used against you.'

They took the screens away to show a dysentery admission. Dennis Plimsolls, a bank manager who wanted to know why he was being arrested for the Drool Post Office robbery. Prune had discharged himself and was even now hobbling home. Never mind he'd get him next time . . .

ARMY DAYS

Looney arose from his reeking bed, his socks adrift on his feet, his shirt *just* covering the family jewels, one arm reached skywards in a luxurious feline stretch revealing the tip.

'Tweak yer willy, sailor,' said the parrot.

'Shut up, yer bastard,' he said, followed by a spasm of bronchial coughing mixed with postern blasts; ever since his army days he always slept in a shirt and socks. Ah, those distant army daze! It wasn't the way to spell it, but that's how he thought it, army daze all now past khaki dream . . .

As a professionally full-time unemployed labourer by trade he had fallen for the blandishments of a recruiting poster: JOIN THE ARMY AND SEE THE WORLD. With war looming, most of them would only see the next. His father had served in the Irish Guards, but then he was over six feet. Now he was under six feet, making a grand total of twelve feet. Looney was only five feet six; still with his father's twelve feet and his five feet six that would make a grand total of seventeen feet six inches! If they wouldn't accept that he could *still* get in! He would *lie* about his height! He'd look powerful good coming home in his busby! People on the tube would stare at him. Mind you, they stared at him now and he wasn't even wearing one. He'd go to local dances wearing it, people would say who's that smart man doing the veleta in a busby?

If there was a war he would try very hard to get the VC, he'd sing 'God Save der King' every day, go to Buckingham Palace and the King would say, 'For devotion to duty and singing 'God Save the King' every day I award you the VC, sign here!' Alas, he never got the VC, but he got close, VD. You could hear his screams from the coast.

143

Promotion! Oh, he'd get that! He'd blanco his rifle and boots so well they'd make him a general, then he could say to his soldiers, 'Kill dat enemy', and they'd *have* to do it, or he'd report them to the police. He'd take them to the dances. People would say, 'Who are those smart men with blancoed rifles and boots wearing busbies doing the veleta?' He'd say, 'They're mine,' and hold up the receipt. Of course *he'd* dress better than his men, *he'd* wear a new evening dress jacket like Henry Hall and his band, London Irish rugby socks, a saffron kilt with patent-leather dance pumps, in case the Queen asked him to veleta. He'd march them home on leave and say, 'For my mudder, presentttttt arms!' If a war came he'd say, 'Good news, fellas . . .'

Strangely, none of it happened like that; his arrived in an envelope marked OHMS. At first he thought it was from the Electricity Board. No, it asked him to report to the Guards depot at Caterham on Monday at fourteen hundred hours. Fourteen hundred? That would be difficult, his watch only went up to twelve.

On the train he asked a fellow passenger, 'Are youse going to join der Irish Guards?'

The man said, 'No,' and Looney said, 'Well, *I am*.'

'No,' said the man, 'I'm not going to join the Irish Guards, I am going to Croydon, Philamore's Fish Shop, you know it?'

'No,' said Looney, 'I'm goin' ter join der Irish Guards.'

'Well,' went on the man, 'I'm going there to get two separate portions of rock salmon and chips. One's for my Auntie Rita, she lives in Revelon Road, you know it?'

'No,' said Looney, 'I'm goin' ter join der Irish Guards.'

'A 13B goes right past the door. You see, she got a double rupture and she's got to stay in bed till the operation, she's on the NHS waiting list. She was very kind to me and my brother Len when we were young, see, we had no bathroom where we lived, that's in 3 Leathwell Road, Deptford, you know it?'

'No,' said Looney.

'A 38 tram stops right by the door.'

'Is dat true?' said Looney.

'Yes, that is true. Why should I lie about a tram? Yes, we

144

used to go to her place on a Friday to have a bath, then she used to live in Catford, 15 Bargery Road, you know it?'

'No,' said Looney. 'What number goes by the door,' he added.

'I don't know, we went by motorcycle and sidecar, yes, she's a tall woman.'

'Who is?' said Looney.

'Auntie Rita, she took me and my brother Len to Hernia Bay on Sunday, I remember it was rainin' so we couldn't go on the beach so she took us to the Rialto Cinema, I remember it was a 244 bus, they were showing Roy Rogers in *Roy Rides West*. (Why would they be showing *Roy Rides West* on a 244 bus? thought Looney) 'Still,' the man continued, 'it was a very misleading title, I mean he couldn't go on riding west otherwise he'd have disappeared off the screen and we'd never have seen him again.'

There the man seemed to stop. Taking advantage, Looney asked the rest of the passengers, 'Excuse me, is anyone here goin' ter join der Irish Guards?' No, no one, fancy dat, fancy a carriage *full* of people and not *one* joining the Irish Guards.

'Mind you, Roy Rogers is not my type of cowboy,' continued the man. 'If I were asked to name cowboy of the year, I'd say Tom Mix ... Did you ever see Buck Jones in *Cimmaron*?'

'No,' said Looney, he'd never even seen him in Kilburn, in any case he was going to join the Irish Guards.

The rectangular sign slowed to a halt by the train window, CATERHA. 'Is dis Caterham?' he said to a passenger.

'Yes, but the M's dropped off.'

Uneasily, Looney left the train. If the M had dropped off, this could be MCATERHA. MCATHERA? The railway porter assured him this wasn't Mcathera but Caterham.

'Der M has dropped off yer sign,' Looney said informatively.

'Yers, I know,' said the porter with that voice that says 'It's dropped off, it has been dropped off for a long time and it's going ter bloody stay dropped orf'. From this attitude sprang British Rail timetables.

Rain started to fall as Looney, carrying his cardboard suitcase, wound his way to the great depot. Gradually the soaking rain permeated the suitcase. Unaware that the bottom half had disintegrated Looney was left clutching the handle. Behind him lay a trail of sock, Razzle, Brylcreem, toothbrush and rosary. At the entrance of the depot he stood before the sign: HQ 2 BATTALION IRISH GUARDS ... QUIS SEPARABIT ... Ah, they've got it in Gaelic as well!

At the gate he was stopped by a gorilla in uniform. 'Oi,' it said, 'where are yew goin'?'

Silly man, Looney wasn't going he was coming. 'I want to join der Second Battalion Quis Separabits.'

The gorilla blinked. 'Wot the fuck are yew talking abaht?' it said.

Looney pointed at the sign. 'I come to join dems,' he smiled.

'Oh,' said the gorilla with an evil grin and a twist of a waxed moustache, 'yew are a very very lucky lad, and we only 'ad one vacancy left, and we bin keeping it for yew! Ha ha ha.'

The gorilla led him to the Medical Officer and rained salutes upon him. 'Mick Rooney reportin' fer duty, SAH!'

The MO Captain Fuller, a regular soldier and military homosexual, said, 'Right, take off your clothes in front of that screen.' Looney stripped under the excited gaze of the officer.

'Now, sit there,' he said. Looney obeyed.

'Jasus, dis seat is bloody cold,' said Looney's bum.

'Now,' said the MO pointing a camera, 'an identification photo for the record. Stand up, bend down and smile,' adding yet another picture to the world's greatest collection of nude guardsmen bending down and smiling. 'How long has it been like that?' said the MO.

'Dat's as long as it's ever been,' said Looney.

Before another officer he was given an oral test. Did he have a police record? No, he had no police record, he had never been in the police. With that they made him sign a piece of paper that implied if he were killed in a war it would be free of charge.

Three weeks and no busby! And all that marching! He *knew* how to walk, he'd learnt when he was only five, by sixteen he had mastered it. It was terrible! He had to salute everybody, even the regimental dog was senior to him. When he stood to attention for it, it pissed down his leg. Why was he suddenly 'Yew 'orrible little nasty man'? But the eight weeks' terrible training had its rewards: he was promoted in the field, Acting Sanitary Orderly second-class. He worked very hard at the latrines and did a good job, as did most of his customers.

Came the war he was very busy, came the bombing he was even busier, but still no busby! How proud he would have been wearing his busby on duty at the latrines; still, there were those women. That knee-trembler Land Girl, what was her name? And that knee-trembler WAAF, what was her name? And that sleazy barmaid in Soho, what was her name? And the burning pain when he did a pee, he knew that name. All now past he came out of the army cured.

Now, today was to be his first day working for that strange Lord O'Goldstein, why didn't he wear any clothes? Perhaps it was an indoor nudist club, so the frost didn't get at them.

THE JASPER McQUONK

Jasper McQuonk was twenty-nine, or was it nineteen? Yes! *Perhaps* he was twenty-nine, or was it sixteen, or all both! That's it, he was all, both twenty-nine, nineteen, twenty and sixteen. The day he was born the parents blamed each other. He grew up a simple boy and sometimes a simple girl. He didn't smoke because he couldn't get the hang of matches; however, he did have the occasional drink, water. He was known in the village as 'There He Goes'. On Guy Fawkes Night his parents built a bonfire for him but he wouldn't go in. They brought him a Doberman pinscher but it failed to kill him.

School was difficult, but only for his teacher. In a zoology lesson Mother Fabian had shown the class a picture of a Hereford bull. 'What is it, children?'

A little girl said, 'It's a cow, miss.'

A little boy: 'A bull.'

Jasper said, 'Hey, look at der balls on dat fella.'

The Bible, Mother Fabian showed an engraving of Adam and Eve in their nakedness.

'Ohhhhhhhhh,' said Jasper. 'Has he been givin' her der old pork sword?' he yokelled.

Arithmetic, Mother Fabian made it easy for him. 'Jasper, a family have two chickens. They eat one, what's left?'

Jasper strained his unicellular brain. 'Bones,' he said.

General knowledge. 'Who did the Allies beat in the last war?'

A little boy said, 'The Germans.'

Mother Fabian looked at Jasper. 'Is that right?'

'Yer,' he said. 'Dey beat der shit out of dem.'

The dear nun blushed with shame. 'Jasper,' she remonstrated, 'you bad bad boy. Write out a hundred times, "I must not say they beat the shit out of them in class".'

'But dey did beat der shit out of dem,' he insisted.

And he was right, they did beat the shit out of them. Was there no truth left in the world? Laboriously he wrote:

1. I mus knot beet thur shit out of thur germans in thur klass room.
2. must I knot beet german shit out of thur klarsroom.
3. I must class the german room ful of shit out of hear.

And so on.

His school report:

English Composition 0
Handwriting 0
Spelling 0
Reading .... 1 (after extra time)
Arithmetic 0

Remarks .... Must try harder

His mother read it. 'Have you seen this?' she said to her husband.

'Oh . . . he dun better dan me,' he said.

A member of the Guild of the Blessed Sacrament taking the collection at church, he handed the plate to the rich Doctor Costello who dropped in a ten pee. 'You mean bugger,' he said in a loud voice.

They tried a child psychiatrist from Dublin. After a week the man was taken away in a straightjacket to marry Zsa Zsa Gabor.

At fifteen Jasper became village errand boy. He delivered goods by forcing them through the letterbox: what started out as a Christmas Pudding ended up a mangled mess on the mat inside. He lived at the bottom of his parents' garden in a converted chicken shed. He was blissfully happy, the converted chicken left. Today he was delivering some jelly to Lord O'Goldstein.

THE LOONEY AND THE CASTLE

It was an apple-green misty morning, everything seemed unreal in the translucent light. Looney shaved in a cracked mirror that made him look like a schizophrenic. It must be terrible to be a schizophrenic. Still, you could go to the pictures alone and not feel alone; at a disco you could go as your own partner.

Why did beards have to grow and yet pubic hairs remained static? Thank God they did. Imagine having to trim them as they hung out of the bottom of your trousers! Supposing women thought it fashionable to *let* them grow. Imagine a honeymoon night, the poor bridegroom saying, 'I give up, dear, where is it?' Mind you, he had been shaved down there, he had been ruptured. Strange, he was only setting a rat trap when it happened.

Waiting for the operation, there was a gentle tap on the door. In came a strapping nurse. 'Good morning,' she shrilled, whipped back the bedclothes, upped with his nightshirt, grabbed his willy, lathered furiously around it till it looked like the Eddystone Lighthouse in a storm, then shaved the whole area till it looked like an oven-ready chicken.

'Excuse me, nurse,' said Looney, 'why did you knock?'

After the operation when the hair started to grow, his willy went through various stages from looking like Bob Geldof to Groucho Marx.

Arriving at the great castle door, Looney pulled the bell stop and heard the bell tintinnabulating down the hall, at which time Puck the clever starling, having dispersed Drool's sheep and sheep dogs across Ireland now proceeded to do his impression of the trim-phone. Looney looked up. Who would put a telephone up a tree? Perhaps it was to make it vandal-proof, or for very tall people? Pulling himself up to the first branch, he swung his leg over. Climbing upwards he ripped his sleeve. He nearly reached the top when, wait! no, it wasn't this tree, it was the next one. Climbing down, he tore the other sleeve, now he had a matching pair. Dropping to the ground, he killed Vernon an ant that was a distant cousin of the one that had nipped his scrotum.

When the castle door was opened, he was up yet a third tree. Mrs Fitts dressed in Spanish flamenco dancer's costume peered out. 'Is somebody there?' she said.

From above a voice answered, 'Yes, I'm up dis tree, mam.'

Peering up, she could see Looney thirty feet above the ground astride a bough inching forward. 'What are you doing up there?' she said.

'I'm answering the phone,' was the reply.

'There's no phone in that tree,' she said. 'It's coming from the hedge!'

Puck now ceased his impression and flew in the direction of some early-morning worms who were about to get the bird.

'Oh it's stopped,' said Looney. 'Dey must ha' got tired of waiting. Shall I wait in case dey rings again?'

'No no no,' said Mrs Fitts. 'We must get on.'

From down the hall Looney could hear a gramophone playing 'The Last Tango in Ireland'.

As he reached the door, she said, 'Your first job is to partner me in 'La Compasita'!' Grabbing his right arm she pulled the sleeve further off. Placing it round her waist she counted him down: 'Four, three, two, one dum-de-dum-dum,' she sang.

Down the long corridor tangoed the ill-matched pair into the kitchen, a vast room with great Gothic vaulted ceilings. A massive kitchen range ran along the wall with a cavernous fireplace for ox or Protestant roasting.

'Your first job,' she said, 'boil an egg.'

Jasus! All dis size ter boil a bloody egg! 'Twas like using tweezers to cut the lawn.

151

'We must hurry! His lordship is waiting. Boil it for three minutes.'

'Where is der egg?' said Looney.

A sly grin spread over her face making an ear-to-ear incision, any more and the top of her head would fall off. 'Ah ha,' she shrilled, clapping her hands together and doing a dodgy pirouette. 'You have to *guess*.'

She wants to play, thought Looney, well, it was better than working. 'It's in der cupboard?'

She shook her head. 'No no no, you have to search.'

'The bread bin?'

'No no no, you're cold.'

Cold? He didn't feel cold and said so. 'I don't feel cold and said so,' he said. Ah! Now he understood, she was giving him clues! When he was red-hot he'd be upon the egg.

The great egg game started, he searched everywhere, he even searched her. 'Jasus, any longer and der bloody ting will hatch,' he complained.

'Give up?' she triumphed. She tangoed to the back door and pointed out. 'In there,' she said, indicating a chicken run.

Entering, Looney was greeted by the disturbed clucking of thirty hens and a deeper clucking from a rooster. One hen was on the nest, but she was asleep. He knew from the encyclopaedia that chickens couldn't lay eggs when they were asleep. Gently prodding her he said, 'Wake up, little birdie.' Under the suspicious gaze of the cockerel, he gently felt under the hen. Please God, no one come in or dey'll tink he was gropin' a chicken. The cockerel gave a loud startling clucking. 'Stop it, you suspicious bastard,' said Looney. The hen suddenly fluttered down from the nest. With every chicken clucking in protest he searched every nest, dis was no job for a King of Ireland . . .

a celtic boiled egg of a day, the fields were heavy wid shillelagh trees, pigs and potato bushes. king looney the one would lay resplendent in his gold workman's hut, his legs heavy with shamrock stickers. he would get up, raise the tail of his shirt and say to the reverend ian paisley. 'right dere!' ian would kiss his lurex wellingtons den start work with a solid-gold bum-

152

scratcher, 'dis could mean promotion for you,' he'd say, and Ian
would say, 'God bless you, sir, lend me a pound or I'll murder yer.'
    Time for his royal egg, he'd get somebody to clap his hands.
'Bring in der royal chicken,' he'd say. In would come Eamonn
Andrews carrying a Rhode Island Red. He'd give the creature a
shake and a squeeze and out would shoot a tree-minute egg
with a gold shell stamped 'Catholic free-range blessed by der
Pope'.

It was a great sight to see the lone Irishman asleep amid thirty
chickens and a cockerel, some of whom were now roosting on
Looney's recumbent figure. Mrs Fitts rattled the door, she
was furious he'd fallen asleep on the job. The last time it
happened to her she pushed him off.

'Wake up,' she shouted, poking him through the wire.
Again it was the first poke he'd had in six months.

'Dere's no eggs,' he said. 'Der chickens must be in der
change.'

'Very well,' said Mrs Fitts, tangoing back into the kitchen,
'it'll have to be these.' She threw a tin of beans.

'Is dere an opener?' he said.

'Yes,' she smiled. 'And it's you.'

Looney found a chopper. Placing the tin on the step, he
tried to perforate the lid.

'Wot you doin'?' said Jasper McQuonk behind him. 'Here,
give me dat chopper.' Taking the tool Jasper raised it and
smashed it down on the tin, splitting it in half amid a shower
of beans.

'Dat's no bloody good,' said Looney. 'Dey's all over der
ground!'

'Soon fix dat,' said McQuonk, scooping a goulash of mud
and beans back into the shattered tin. 'Well,' he said, 'dat's
my good deed fer der day,' and left.

THE BLESSING

Father Costello had come by holy Catholic bicycle to bless the cottage. 'You said it wasn't urgent, Mrs Looney,' he said.

'That's right, Fadder, I wanted you ter bless it before it fell down.' She led him in and opened the door to the kitchen, a sea of smoke met his eyes. ''Tis the chimney, Fadder,' coughed Mrs Looney. 'You can see how badly der place needs blessing. Will youse have a drink?'

Coughing, the priest sat at the table. Coughing, she poured a glass of whiskey. As the drink tinkled into the glass, there was the sound of thudding footsteps approaching from the garden. In rushed Looney himself.

'Ah,' he coughed. 'I thought I heard whiskey and coughing,' he said, selecting another glass. 'Nice ter see you, Fadder.'

'I'm sorry, I can't see you,' coughed the priest through the smoke.

Father Costello could see that not only had he been painting the house but apparently also himself. The man's face was splattered with white. Father Costello placed a bottle of holy water on the smoke-obscured table. Mistakenly Looney opened it and filled his glass. Vaguely through the smoke Father saw a glass appear at the end of an arm.

'Cheers, Fadder,' said coughing, smoke-shrouded Looney. 'Yes, I bin paintin' der outside, dat's der side dat people see first.'

'I see,' coughed Father Costello who now couldn't see anything.

Looney went silent as he drank the holy water, God, dis was cheap stuff.

'Are you still there, Mrs Looney?' coughed the priest.

'Yes, I'm in there somewhere,' she coughed, and he coughed, 'I must get on with the blessing.'

He stood and mistakenly picking up the whiskey bottle started to sprinkle it round the house intoning, 'God bless this house dear, and make the chimney better. May the blessing of our Lord Jesus Christ come on this house and increase its market value.'

Ah Jesus, thought Looney, dere was a fine man, if he'd have been Jesus dem bloody Protestant Romans would never have got him . . .

THE SHAMROCK GOLGOTHA

. . . The sky was an octopus-ink black. It was chilly as the Roman soldier kept his lonely vigil by the three stark crosses. He cupped his hands and blew a draught of warm air into them. Where was his relief? The tramp of hobnailed sandals announced his arrival, Private Prescribus Vallium. 'Hello, Ancillius, sorry I'm late, my candle was slow.'

' 'Salright,' said Ancillius.

'Anything to report?'

Ancillius drew his cloak around him. 'No, nuffink. There's some mulled wine in the guardroom.'

'Ah, lovely, see you tomorrow,' he said. With his spear at the trail Prescribus walked into the engulfing darkness, his footsteps the only sound breaking the night. He stationed himself at the foot of the central cross, then he heard 'Pssst'. He peered into the dark. 'Pssssssssssstt!' it came again. 'Up here,' said a voice. Prescribus ran his eyes across the three crucified figures. 'It's me up here.'

Was he imagining? He moved to the foot of the middle cross. 'Did you say something?' he said, addressing the figure in the kilt.

'Yes,' he said.

Prescribus took a step forward. 'You're supposed to be dead,' he said. 'What do you want?'

The figure moved. 'I've had enough,' said Looney.

'No, you haven't,' said Prescribus. 'When you're dead you've had enough.'

'I tell you,' said Looney, 'I want der nails out.'

Prescribus was aghast. 'You want the nails out?' he repeated.

'Yes,' said Looney.

'You'll fall off and kill your bloody self,' said Prescribus.

'I want to come down,' said Looney.

Prescribus smacked his thigh. 'Ouch, you must be daft! It's more than my job's worth.'

'I want . . .' said Looney.

'No no,' said the soldier. 'No more I wants, you've been sentenced to death, so go to sleep!'

Sleep up here? Was he joking? 'Listen,' said Looney. 'I was sentenced to death for sayin' I was King of der Jews.'

'Well?' said the soldier.

'Well,' said Looney, 'I've recanted, I'm *not* der King of der Jews, I'm an Irish one!'

'You should have said that at the trial.'

'Well, it was all so quick, der jury was rigged, it was full of Pakistanis, I got confused, I didn't have a solicitor or time to mull it over.'

Prescribus paused. 'Well, what do you want me to do about it?'

'I told you, I want der nails out, I've *said* I'm not King of the Jews, haven't I?'

Prescribus banged his spear down on the rocks. 'It's no good sayin' it to me. I'm just an ordinary squaddie.' The cheek of the man!

'Well,' went on Looney, 'if you get me down I'll say it to someone more important.'

'Listen, if I took you down I'd be court martialled!'

'You don't want an innocent man's death on your conscience, I mean youse do believe me.'

'Yes, oh dear, this puts me in a very difficult position.'

'Well, what do you think I'm in?'

'I can't do it, mate.'

'Who's your superior.'

'It's Centurion Appalonius.'

'Well, let me talk to him.'

'You mean . . . wake him up????'

'Well, you can't talk while you're asleep.'

'Look, not him, he's a bastard. I'll call the Guard Commander Sergeant Titus.'

The soldier walked briskly away. Looney waited: he'd fool this lot, he'd get away. Prescribus returned with the sergeant buckling on his breastplate.

'This soldier says you want the nails out because you've recanted.'

'Yes, Sergeant, I want to tell Pontius Pilate I'm sorry, I'm not the King of the Jews.'

'Well, you've set us a problem.'

'Problem? All you need is a pair of pliers.'

The sergeant rubbed his chin. 'Yes yes, but the regimental carpenter's shop closed at six, he's the only one who's got a pair.'

Looney didn't say anything for a time, the two soldiers looked up at him. Finally he spoke. 'What time does he open his shop in the morning?'

'Seven o'clock,' said Prescribus.

'Can you wait till then?' said the sergeant.

A note of annoyance crept into Looney's voice. 'Wait till then? That's nine hours up here. I'll never last der night, the weather forecast says heavy frosts.'

The sergeant stroked his chin again. 'Supposin' we get you an overcoat.'

Looney let out a guffaw, 'Don't be silly, how am I goin' ter get an overcoat on over dis lot!'

All three's attention was drawn by approaching footsteps. From the dark came a patrolling Jewish nightwatchman. ''Ello, 'ello, 'ello, wot's goin' on 'ere?' he said.

'Ah, constable,' said the sergeant, 'maybe you can help. He's recanted and wants to come down.'

'Oh.' The watchman looked up. 'He's *not* the King of the Jews?' he queried.

'No, he says no.'

The nightwatchman took out a notebook. 'Well, he's within his rights, he can ask for a retrial.' He looked up at Looney. 'You picked a very awkward time, it's Shabus, everywhere, but everywhere is closed.' He turned to the sergeant. 'Are the other two dead?'

Prescribus nodded.

158

'Oh,' said the watchman pointing at Looney, 'they were giving odds that 'e would go first.' He looked up at Looney. 'You know you were 7 to 4 favourite.'

'Yes, I'll tell my father to put it all on the nose.'

'A lot of punters are going to be very disappointed with you.'

'Oh yes? Who wants friends that want you dead!'

Prescribus interjected, 'They expected you to die for them as a martyr.'

'All right, a martyr but not this way. I promise I'll die for them again.'

'How?'

'Bronchitis.'

'How's that going to look in print? To wash away the sins of the world he died of bronchitis!'

'Never mind all that, please get me down. I'm starting to get cold, they're all shrivelled up.'

'We keep saying we haven't got the tools!'

'My father Joseph, he's a chippy, he'll give you a pair. Number Seven Via Dolorosa, just down there on the right.'

The two Romans whispered in conference. 'All right,' they agreed.

Good, thought Looney, he'd soon be down and off to Australia.

'I suppose you get a good view from up there,' said the nightwatchman.

Prescribus returned with Joseph. 'My son, my son,' he bewailed.

'Hello, Dad, I'm sorry to do this to you.'

'They tell me you want to come down.'

'Yes.'

'How long for?'

'How long? For good!'

'You know what you're doing!'

'What do youse mean, do I know what I'm doing? Nailed up here I can't do anything.'

Wearily Joseph placed the ladder against the cross. 'I'll take 'em out of your feet, otherwise you'll go head first.'

It took five minutes. Looney followed him down the ladder. 'I brought these sandals and this cloak.' Gratefully he wrapped it around himself. 'I'll get some Elastoplast over dese holes.'

'Is it all right if I spend der night at me dad's house? All me stuff is there.'

The sergeant sucked in his breath. 'All right, all right, but you got to report to the guardroom tomorrow first thing.'

'First ting,' said Looney. Taking the end of the ladder, he followed his father.

Out of earshot, Joseph spoke, 'You see, son, you put us all in a spot. Everyone in Jerusalem takes it that you're dead. We got all the embalming fluids, the shroud, paid a deposit on the tomb and we laid on all the food and wine for the funeral, all that.'

'Don't worry, Dad, I got a plan,' said Looney as they reached the house.

'Oh, my son, my son,' said Mary. 'I've got some Irish stew waiting for you.'

The three sat eating at the table drinking poteen. Looney unfolded his master plan. It was simple, they need change nothing. 'When dey comes to collect me in der morning, I'm going to feign death. You wrap me up and stitch me in dat holy shroud of Turin, den when der Romans come you say I died in the night, den you go through wid der funeral, take me to der tomb and put der rock against der hole. When it's dark I'll do a bunk and leave a local actor in a white sheet wearing wings ter say "He has arisen". By den I'll be on my way to Australia, and youse tell der press I've ascended into heaven, den you get der cross, saw it up and start sellin' der bits . . .'

THE LOONEY AND THE REWARD

'SLimMinG DisseaSe girl is VANisheS

Looney sat up in bed and read, read, re-read the *Drool Bugle*. Bit by bit it was gradually going in, but almost immediately coming out again. It needed a stone mason to engrave every word into his brain – his memory wasn't going, it hadn't even arrived. 'Dis says dat a 1/4 horse calleD Sherbert A has been stoled from its=staible£.'

Across the room Mrs Looney knelt in prayer before a clockwork statue of the Virgin Mary from Hong Kong that whistled Ave Maria every hour on the hour.

'Did youse hear dat?' said Looney from his reeking bed.

She ignored him intoning, 'HailMaryfullofgracetheLordis-withthee . . .'

Freeing one hand from the paper, Looney dove it under the blankets and set about vigorous itinerant scratching, producing a muffled sound. 'Ohhhhhh, listen to dis,' scratch scratch, 'der Polis ist offerung a tousand $ pounds for der reTurn of der horse,' scratch scratch, 'did you hear dat, darlin'?'

Yes, she heard it and it sounded as if he was tearing the skin off. 'Blessed art thou,' she droned. 'Can't youse see I'm praying – among women and blessed is –' she was interrupted by the parrot on his perch viewing the world from the best position, upside down. 'Tweak yer willy, sailor,' he squawked. 'Shut up, yer bastard,' she said. 'Holy Mary Mother of God pray for us and ask yer son to let us win the pools.'

Looney read again: 'It says dis1/4stallion is worth' – here he gasped – 'ONE MILLION%POUNDS! Jasus, how could a *horse* save dat much?' There was a description: 'chestknut

161

cooler, may only have tree legs'! Well, he'd keep his eyes, ears and nose and throat open for the creature. Three legs eh? He swung his two legs over the side of the bed plunging one in the po, dousing his sock. 'Darlin'! Will youse *not* leave der po stickin' out like dis!' he wailed.

'It's not to go under der bed,' she said.

'Oh? And why not?'

'Because the steam rusts der springs.'

Now, how did she find dat out? She must ha' been under dare wid an inspection lamp.

The morning rain had stopped, the sun shone and the land steamed ankle-high. Cows floated on the mirage as Looney took a short cut to the castle. 'If you iver go across der sea to Ireland,' he sang, 'den maybe at the closin' of der day.' By Gor he sounded like Bing Crosby dat American singing golfer. If his voice had been a pound note it would have been the greatest forgery ever.

As he sang on, Looney passed the foot of Maughan Hill with its Iron Age fort alone with its ghosts of the Fir Bolg. Somewhere up there, his predecessors had stood hand in hand against the Danes and bailiffs. His attention was taken by the whinny of a horse, a horse!!! A thousand pounds if it had tree legs. Peering through the hedge he saw it. Oh bugger! Four legs! Just *one* out! How near he'd been! Still, it was the wrong colour, black. He walked and sang on: 'You can sit and watch the sun riseeeeeeeeeeeeeeee over Cavannnnnnnnnnnnnnnnnnn.' Wait, was he *sure* it had four legs? He turned to double check. This time the horse was white with four legs. Still, you can't win 'em all, but on reflection he recalled he'd never won any, even this new job, it said five pounds a week all found and so far he hadn't found anything.

'Please God,' he said out loud, 'please let der next horse be a tree-legged one and while you're on it, can you up the reward?'

'Is that all you think abaht?' said God.

'Ah, God,' said Looney, lighting a fag. 'I'm glad youse heard dat, where are youse?' he said, looking up and down and around and each ways everywhere.

162

'I'm here in this burning bush,' said God emerging from it.

'Youse lucky you don't get scorched doin' dat,' said Looney. But, oh God! What a disappointment, he was dressed as a fireman. 'What's dis den?' said Looney, pointing to the uniform.

'Oh, that,' said God apologetically, 'well, Mick, you see I'm divine, I'm like a ball of light ten times as bright as the sun.'

'Is dat right?'

God nodded, 'Yes, well, I couldn't come down to earth like that, could I? I mean, how could I have gone into Sainsbury's like that? No, I had to take human shape, so I resurrected the body of a fireman killed in the Blitz, Charlie Ward from 'Ackney, that's why I'm torkin' Cockney.'

Looney smiled. 'Youse won't find many fires ter put out here.'

'Oh, good,' said God, 'I'm not into fires, miracles are more my line.'

'Oh, well den,' said Looney, 'do der loaves and der fishes, den we can have lunch.'

'Oh no, I can only do those when I'm God.'

'What *can* you do, den?' said Looney.

God laughed. 'Put out fires,' he said.

Looney opened his tin. 'Would youse like a cigarette?'

God shook his head. 'No, I don't want to start at my time of life. Any case, you can't get 'em where I come from, but we get a lot of 'em comin' up who did, that's how they got there.'

'Is it crowded?' said Looney.

God shook his head woefully. 'Yer, 'fraid so, packed aht like Heathen, they're sleeping six to a room.'

'Are dey Pakistanis?' said Looney.

'Oh no,' said God.

Looney looked at his watch. Jasus, he'd be late. 'Got ter go, but I'll be at der pub tonight if you fancies a jar.'

They shook hands and God disappeared, back into the burning bush. Oh! thought Looney, he must carry a lot of fire insurance.

The talk with God the fireman had delayed him, he quickened his pace. He passed a tree with its telephone

163

ringing, he hadn't time to answer it. When he arrived at the castle door he was twenty minutes late, that or the castle was twenty minutes early. Just in case he put his watch back twenty minutes then to make up the time rang the great doorbell quickly. It opened on the great Mrs Fitts in a Charleston costume.

'It's the Black Bottom today,' she said.

'Oh,' said Looney. 'Let's have a look.'

She then danced him to the kitchen in a frenzied Charleston. 'Why are you late?' she said.

'I stopped to talk with God the fireman.'

'That's no excuse,' she said, 'but it's most original. Next week Lord O'Goldstein is having a Guy Fawkes Night.'

Looney interrupted, 'Dat's not till November der Fifth.'

'Tsu,' she said, 'in the Jewish calendar it's September, when the fireworks are cheaper.'

'Oh,' said he.

'Everyone is coming in fancy dress,' she said.

Looney groaned. 'Fancy dress? Fancy dat.' He didn't fancy dat. 'Dis is the only clothes I'se got.'

She eyed him up and down. 'You can go as a shit house. Now, the fireworks in the woodshed, put them all in the yard.'

There was something nasty in the woodshed; Looney trod in it. Fireworks! Hundreds of pounds' worth. All afternoon he laboured and stacked them in a mountainous pile in the yard.

From a turret window came a wail. 'Sanctuaryyyyyyyyyy, sanctuary' – it was the crazed haired-black demented son of Lord O'Goldstein, alias the Hunchback of Notre Drool. Lowering a rope from the window, it slid down to the smell of burning flesh, hairs and screams. 'Esmerelda, have you seen Esmerelda? If they touch her anywhere from the waist down, I want the negatives. Here,' he handed Looney a trouser button, 'a groat, keep your silence.' The hunchback lolloped off to answer a phone call in that tree.

At five o'clock Mrs Fitts called in Looney for a cup of tea, a bottle of brandy and the Boston Two-Step. 'Has anybody told you you're a good dancer?' she said.

164

'Yes,' he said.

'Well,' she said, 'they're bloody liars.'

So ended Looney's first week at the castle being paid in five pounds still bearing George V's face. O'Goldstein was a slow spender.

> Water does not stay in a sieve,
> Nor gold in a generous pocket.
> *Old Proverb*

By ten that night Looney was pissed and broke.

THE DECAY

The gods send nuts to those who have no teeth,
They also send teeth to those who have no nuts.
Old Irish Proverb

Looney inserted his top dentures with a noise like ivory dice rattling in a cup. Worse, his back molar had decay, he couldn't understand it, he brushed them regularly . . . once a month. The dentist in Limerick was the nearest dentist. In his pocket Looney carried his wife's shopping list. He caught a country bus.

'Do youse go ter Limerick?' he said to the conductor.

'I have to,' said the man desperately. 'This bus goes there.'

Looney placed himself next to a middle-aged woman, about sixteen hundred AD, he thought; on her lap she carried a wicker basket.

'Fares, please,' said the conductor.

'Limerick,' said Looney.

'Dat will be seventy pee,' said the conductor.

'*Seventy* pee? Don't youse know a shorter route?'

From the basket came a plaintive mewing.

'Is dat a pussycat you got in dere?'

She smiled – *she* should be going to the dentist. 'Yes,' she said, sending out a wave of day-later onions. 'It's a tom, I'm takin' him for the operation.'

Poor little bugger, havin' his knackers nipped off. Those people who believed in reincarnation had a lot to answer for – why, that could be the late Frédéric Chopin in that basket! A terrible ting ter cut der balls of der man who invented der Nocturnes. 'What colour is he?'

Another wave of ageing onions as she said, 'Black.'

166

Oh, a nigger, den it couldn't be Chopin, Chopin wasn't a nigger, so it might be dat poor nigger Duke Ellington, der hot banjo player and singer of coon songs. Reincarnation, if he came back he'd like to be der Pope.

His holiness Pope Looney the First was kneeling in the Sistine Chapel blessing his overdraft. When he'd done that he announced promotions: Wogan would become blessed Terry; his mother would become a saint along with the London Irish Rugby Club and George Best; he'd invite Joan Collins and after doing the Vatican Veleta he'd bless her sex life and TV series; Reagan would ask his advice and he'd say, 'Ronald, drop der bomb on dem bloody Russians or put ten pounds in der poor box,' then he'd sing Ave Maria to Reagan free of charge.

The bus conductor was shaking him awake. 'Did you want to get off at Limerick?'

'Yes,' said Looney.

'It's a mile back there,' said the conductor.

In drenching rain Looney started to walk, rain ran through his clothes trickling down his body, conduited by his legs, collecting in pools in his boots then artistically squirting through the lace holes like the fountains of Rome by Respighi. Dat bastard bus conductor! When he was der King of Ireland he'd never have stood for dis . . .

'BRING DER BUGGER IN,' ROARED KING LOONEY THE JUST.

TWO MASSIVE NEGRO SLAVES IN SHAMROCK LOINCLOTHS DRAGGED THE BUS CONDUCTOR SCREAMING FROM HIS BUS. THE KING RIPPED THE TICKET MACHINE FROM HIS GRASP AND PLACED IT ON AN ANVIL. A GIANT RAGING WITH MUSCLES AND BLACK HAIRS RAISED A MOWLEMS SLEDGEHAMMER AND SMASHED THE MACHINE TO BITS. 'EAT DAT,' HE SAID TO THE BUS CONDUCTOR. WITH THE SMASHING OF TEETH, HE SWALLOWED IT ALL AND GROANED, 'YOU'LL GET ME DER SACK.' SCREAMING, HE WAS PLACED ON A TREADMILL WITH A CASCADING SHOWER OVERHEAD. 'IT'S BLOODY FREEZING.'

THE KING LAUGHED. 'LIKE DAT FOCKIN' RAIN EH?' ANOTHER SIGNAL AND THE TREADMILL REVOLVED. 'START WALKIN', YER BASTARD.'

WITH THE BUS CONDUCTOR'S LEGS DOING FIFTY MILES AN HOUR AND HIS BODY TAKING A THOUSAND GALLONS OF WATER A MINUTE, THERE CAME THE ORDER, 'PUT HIS BALLS IN A RAT TRAP.' THEN THE WORST TORTURE OF ALL!

'SMILE,' SAID THE KING AS THE TRAP SNAPPED SHUT.

By the time the bus conductor's balls were secured in the

rat trap he had reached Limerick. Entering a pub, he ordered a Jameson.

'Do you want ice?' said the barman.

'Ice? Ice?' he said. 'Man, did youse not know what it did to der Titanic?'

'I was never on it,' said the barman.

He looked at his shopping list, baked beans, one jam roll, right. It was a small shop. 'How much are two tins of beans?' he said to the little shopkeeper.

'One pound, sir,' he said.

'How much is one?'

'Sixty pee.'

'Den I'll have the other one. Now, how much is two jam rolls?'

'One pound fifty.

'How much is one?'

'Ninety-four pee.'

'Den I'll have der other one.'

'That *is* the other one, sir,' said the little shopkeeper who had wised up.

Carrying his purchases in a plastic bag, Looney entered the rain-filled streets to the dentist's waiting-room. Sopping, he sat in a vacant seat. Around, against the walls like living tombstones, were some ten people awaiting the dental onslaught. Thank God the room had a coal fire; he didn't thank God when he started to steam . . . waves of it rose from his clothes until he was obscured in a white mist.

A small child in a loud voice said, 'Look, Mum, that man is melting.'

The mother shushed the child. 'No, dear, he's only steaming . . .'

'Why is he steaming?' said the child in a loud voice.

'Because all his clothes are wet.' She smiled at Looney.

'Why is he wet and we're dry?' said the child in a loud voice.

'Because, dear, the man didn't have an umbrella.'

Looney moved uneasily as the rest of the room used him as the cabaret.

168

'Can't he afford an umbrella, Mummy?' said the child in a loud voice.

'Shhhhh, child. Perhaps he left it at home,' said the mother.

'He must be stupid to leave it when it's raining.'

'Shhhhh, child.'

Ohhh, if he were the Kind of Ireland . . .

king looney aimed his blunderbuss loaded with crap and killed the child stone dead in a loud voice.

Looney read one of the waiting-room papers. It was terrible news! the R101 had crashed! Outside, below the dental studio, navvies started to work, there came the sound of a pneumatic drill followed by a scream from the surgery. Christ! thought Looney as he watched people scramble from the room, he was now the last patient.

'There's only one left,' the nurse informed the dentist as his phone rang. It was the wife, would Daddy say goodnight to Sandra before she went to bed. 'Hel-lo, Daddee,' said the five-year-old. 'Can you do that doggy noise?'

When Looney entered, it was to the dentist barking down the phone. The dentist gave an embarrassed smile. 'Just saying goodnight to my daughter.'

'What is she?' said Looney. 'A cocker spaniel, ha ha ha.'

I'll get him for this, thought the dentist. 'Say ahhhh.' He inserted a mirror and a probe. 'What appears to be the trouble?'

'Argggg gargggg gorddddd abraggggg,' said Looney. He inserted a finger and identified the tooth. The dentist plunged the probe shoulder deep into the cavity. Looney screamed.

'Is that it?' gloated the dentist. 'Just give you a pain-killing injection,' he laughed, and plunged a hypodermic into the gum.

'Arghhhhhhhhhhhhh!' screamed Looney. 'Any deeper and you'll stroike focking oil!'

'Quiet,' shouted the dentist. 'You'll ruin the bloody business.'

Looney fainted. With great expertise the dentist removed

the wrong tooth – it is a medical fact that bad eyesight can cause loss of teeth. Gradually Looney came to. 'Ohhh, where am I?' he said.

'Limerick,' said the dentist, 'and that will be five pounds.' Again Looney fainted.

When he came round again they were feeling for the money in his pockets. 'We weren't sure you'd come back,' said the dentist.

In bed that night the king of Ireland strapped the dentist to a bed of electrified nails, stood on the dentist's chest, put his foot under his chin and pulled his teeth out one by one with a pair of red-hot pliers, then applied the traditional rat trap to his scrotum and said, 'dat'll be five pounds.'

THE INSPECTOR CALLS

Inspector McTruss drove to the car park behind Drool Garda station, braked, and the mudguard fell off. Replacing the string, he entered the rear entrance. But first a photograph, every clue counted. At the back door he was stopped by Garda O'Brien with a duck on a lead.

'What in God's name is dis supposed to be, man?' he enquired. 'Fattening it up fer Christmas, ha ha ha!'

No, O'Brien was not fattening it up for Christmas. He explained, 'Dis is an experimental securi-duck.'

McTruss burst out laughing and a button flew off his waistcoat. 'Is it a joke?'

'No, sir,' said O'Brien. 'It's a securi-duck. You see, the police dog died and with the price of dog food rocketing it was estimated that to keep a duck was a lot cheaper.'

'Well, what do you feed him on?' said McTruss.

'We feed him on that bit of waste ground over there,' said O'Brien, pointing to the rest of Ireland. 'He's very good and alert, he quacks at anyone approaching.' O'Brien went on to point out that the duck also laid eggs and at the end of his tour of duty supplied them with a good dinner.

Ah well, thought McTruss, if the humble goose saved Rome, then the duck could save Drool. Sergeant Kelly showed him a map of the area search for Sherbert. McTruss showed him his holiday snaps of Majorca. Now first a photo of him in front of the map and next standing next to the securi-duck, every clue counted.

'Do you think this is the work of one man or a gang?' said Sergeant Kelly.

'Yes,' said McTruss, 'I think it's the work of one man or a gang.'

'Are there any suspects?' said Kelly.

'Oh yes,' said McTruss, 'there are plenty of suspects, right now I don't know who they are.'

There's an old Irish saying and he was it.

THE LONG AND
THE SHORT

Why why why and why was he of Irish royal blood and only five feet six inches? Every inch a king? Then he had not enough inches: a king should be inches of more inches, at least six feet five inches of inches. Mind you, he might have been just that had it not been for the smoking. 'Dat stunted me growths,' said Looney. Mind you, he knew a midget who *didn't* smoke and he was only four feet; mind you, if he *had* smoked, today that midget would only be, say, two feet nine inches and a doorstep. Then again, he knew Tim Muldoon the circus giant who was nine feet ten and he smoked! Mind you if he *hadn't* smoked today he could be nineteen feet ten inches and a thriving window cleaner. No, it was never too late to kick the habit. Looney himself *would* stop *now*.

That night he measured himself against the bathroom wall and made a mark. All night long he didn't smoke. Next morning he was still the same height. As a five-foot-six-inch king, he would have to make height laws so tall people couldn't look down on him. As a precaution he would always carry a royal ladder in case! But at the same time he would divide his kingdom up into areas: in his palace he would only employ midgets and dwarfs under three feet – that would give him a commanding lead – and in the surrounding area he would only allow five-foot-five people.

the royal height warden was giving evidence. 'on october the turd, your majesty, i saw der accused dominic behan, being five feet nine in a royal five feet six area i cautioned him and told him he was exceeding the royal height limit by inches three. later dat day i saw him again in a five foot tree area, this time being six feet inches one, exceeding the height by inches seven. i put the height clamp on him and took him to a five feet six police station.'

the king spoke from the top of the ladder. 'dominic behan, mensurationist extraordinary, have you anything to say?'

'yes, sire,' said behan. 'i got drunk and i lost control of me height.'

king looney put on the black crown. 'then, dominic behan, i sentence you to be sent to a reduction chamber and there steamed until you are only one foot seven inches.'

THE LOONEY, THE HORSE, THE CHILDREN, THE CASTLE

On his way now to Lord O'Goldstein's castle, Looney was passing two children on a great white horse. Curses! They were looking *down* on him, it was those extra horse inches.

'Mister,' says the girl, 'will you help us down?'

'How did you get on?' said Looney.

'We get on very well,' said the children.

The horse turned round into a black one. 'What happened to the udder one?' said baffled Looney. 'This is the other one,' said the boy as Looney lowered him to the ground. Now they would both have to look *up* to him and his inches. Jasus! Der horse was half black and half white!! A nigger father! He gave the creature a scrumped apple. The apple contained a little worm called Eric. After a long dark period, Eric would surface on a road in reduced circumstances. 'Goodbye,' said the children, leaving him with the horse, an apple freak.

Looney was on his way, then, a smile, a song and a prolapse, followed by the horse. Unaware, he sang, 'Ohhhhhhh, I love the dear silver that shines in your teethhhhhhh.' The horse nuzzled him for another apple. 'Shoo, go away,' he said to no avail, he also said it to the horse. All his life Looney had followed the horses, now one was following him. Coming up the opposite way was the fast hobbling figure of Rory Prune, fleeing from O'Brien.

'Ah, hello dere,' said Looney.

'I niver seed dat horse in my life,' said Prune. ''Tis a lie and I'm innocent of der Post Office robbery,' said Prune, increasing his speed to ten hobbles an hour, and he shouted back down the road, 'I didn't know der girl was under tirteen.'

What a strange fella! thought Looney. If I had a broken leg I wouldn't take it out fer walks, jest to tell people I didn't know der girl was under tirteen.

At the entrance to the castle the stable lad became very unstable. That horse with Looney! It was the living image of Sherbert. It was in fact identically identical but for the fact it wasn't. If it had been brown instead of sometimes black and sometimes white it would have been even identicaller except that it wasn't otherwise yet! 'Is dat your horse, mister?' said the lad.

Looney had a think. 'Perhaps,' he said. It was as good an answer as any, it wasn't as positive as yes, but less negative than no. At which moment, a flock of terrified sheep raced down the road chased by a sheepdog with a whistling starling overhead, followed in turn by a shepherd at 200 to 1 firing a shotgun and screaming, 'Bernard-Paul-George-Ringo-Boy! Come here, you bastard!'

'Can I stick me horse in here?' said Looney, leading it into Sherbert's stall.

'Yes,' said the boy, 'you'll find the glue on the shelf.'

Mrs Fitts was waiting at the castle door. Looney caught her in flagrante delicto stuffing balloons up the back of the Hunchback of Notre Dool, née Drool. 'The boy keeps bursting them, Mr Looney,' she wailed as she cha-chaed him to the kitchen.

Standing in a zinc bath, his trousers rolled up, peeling potatoes, was a dark-skinned man with piercing black eyes very close to the bridge of his nose – when he glanced sideways one eye appeared to cross over. 'This is Fred Vahey,' she said. 'He's a tinker.'

A tinker, eh? I wonder what he's tinkin right now, thought Looney.

'Help him peel the tatties.'

Looney took up a knife. Together they peeled in silence, save the odd whistling noise in the key of C that came from the tinker's nose.

176

'Tell me, why has you got yer trousers rolled up?' said Looney.

'I tn'did tnaw ot teg ym sresuort tew,' said the tinker.

'Wot's dat?' said Looney.

The tinker louder said, 'I TN DID TNAW OT TEG YM SRESUORT TEW.'

'Is dis fella a foreigner?' said Looney.

'No, he's dyslexic,' she said, winding the horned gramophone and putting on the late John McCormack. 'I'llll meet her in the garden where the praties grow gr-ow gr-ow gr-ow gr-ow gr-ow.' She slid the needle forward across John McCormack's throat.

'Coo-eee!' the voice of Lord O'Goldstein, high on sexual adrenalin and Horlicks, came through the kitchen door keyhole.

'What is it, me lud?' she said.

'Red jelly doesn't give me a hard-on any more, Mrs Fitts.'

'Then,' said Mrs Fitts, 'then the doctor says we must change to white blancmange and increase the massage.'

The keyhole groaned, 'I think I might be in the homosexual menopause.'

Mrs Fitts turned John McCormack over. 'I've been through the homosexual menopause,' she said. 'I'm currently going through the lesbian one.'

'Bingo!' said the keyhole. O'Goldstein wandered off wondering if sleeping alone was contagious.

THE HUNT BALLS

The perverted costumed guests arrived in dribs and drabs. Dey got to arrive in something, thought Looney, now resplendent in a flunkey's outfit two sizes too large, his head just appearing now and then like an emerging tortoise. He stood at the ballroom entrance announcing each arrival by character: two Romans, 'Mister and Missus Julius Kaiser'; a one-eyed sailor, 'Lord and Missus Horatio Neilson'; 'Mr Saint Francis of Issisey', 'James Blonde, 009', and so on.

In the minstrels gallery Mrs Sheena Kilroy, aged seventy-one, led her even older Drool Quartet of Viols in a desperate attempt at the latest dance tune they knew, 'Where's that tiger?' The febrile sound bounced around the giant ballroom echoing and re-echoing off the walls.

What a mean bugger that Lord O'Goldstein was, thought Looney. Wid his money you'd ha' tought he could ha' afforded a bigger quartet dan dis. The guests were partaking of Mrs Fitts' punch, a concoction of poteen, whiskey, champagne and Galloways' Lung Syrup. Very soon its potency imposed itself on the depraved gathering. 'Oh dear,' said a homosexual Queen Victoria, 'I must lie down, I've come over all queer.' It now lay asleep on a couch. One by one the others collapse: Disraeli, then Lord Kitchener, Anna and the King of Siam, all distributed around the room in the supine position.

From a centrally placed cupboard a groan of ecstasy came through the keyhole while inside O'Goldstein massaged his jelly, as whirling past went a gay Kaiser of Germany clutching a bi-sexual Catherina of the Russias. The central cupboard was over-vibrating and crashed forward trapping the good lord inside. Giggling guests lifted it upright; Lord O'Goldstein emerged with a squashed jelly.

'Mr Looney,' shrilled Mrs Fitts, dressed as Isadora Drunken, 'a fresh jelly for his lordship! A greennnn one!' It was to be a long hard day for Looney.

THE TRACTOR RIDE

While Looney laboured at the castle, his brother Shamus Looney's tractor chugged merrily towards the potato field. Skeins of morning mist interwove in the hedgerows, the sun was breaking the horizon, he heard the last of the dawn chorus. Shamus's tractor turned into the fallow field as time-trained gulls flocked in his wake to partake of fresh-churned worms. Above the chug of the engine, Shamus sang an old Irish jig:

> Ohhhhh, you dirty old devil how dare you presume
> To pee in the bed when the po's in the room.
> I'll wallop yer filthy old bum with a broom
> When I get up in the morning timeeeeeeeeeeee.

Shamus set the tractor in line to plough the first furrow. As the ploughshare sank into the yielding earth, the gulls rose in a cloud like a benediction of white feathers, their raucous hymns vying with the tractor's noise – a collision of nature and technology. Halfway along the first furrow a man stepped out of the hedgerow to thumb a lift; it was Jasper McQuonk, ace Drool delivery boy.

Halting the tractor, Shamus shouted, 'What is it lad?'

The lad grinned. 'Any chance of a lift?' he said.

'A lift,' puzzled Shamus. 'God, man, we're in a field, where is it you're going?'

'Well, where are *you* going?'

'Up to der end and den back again.'

McQuonk touched his hat with his index finger in a salute. 'Dat'll do me fine.'

So saying, he climbed up into the cab.

The tractor chugged on. 'I'm out for a nice long walk,' said McQuonk, grinning.

'A walk?' said Shamus. 'Jasus, man, dis isn't walkin'!'

McQuonk gave an idiot laugh. 'What good's walkin' when you're on a tractor?'

Shamus gave a bemused smile. 'Walkin' gets you from A to B,' he said. 'Where's B?' said McQuonk.

'Well, dat's just a term. Supposin' here is A, when we get to der end, dat's B.'

This temporarily silenced McQuonk, who sat grinning at the world while sucking a boiled sweet with the wrapping still on.

The tractor arrived at the end of the first furrow and started to turn. 'Is dis B?' said McQuonk.

'Yes,' said Shamus. 'I never been to B before,' said McQuonk. 'Do you ever go to C or D or E?'

No, Shamus had never been to C, D or E.

What was Shamus ploughing for?

Potatoes.

'Ohhhhh, potatoes,' said McQuonk, with awe in his voice, 'I like potatoes. Guess what, I' – here McQuonk poked himself in the chest – 'I know how to eat potatoes . . . not just one, but lots, three, four, twelve.' He went on poking himself with his finger. Alas, it would be the only poke he would ever have.

By now the tractor had arrived back at A. 'I'll get off here, please,' said McQuonk and leapt from the cab, landing amid a snowstorm of gulls who rained spots on his overcoat. 'Tanks for der lift.'

Shamus drove on and sang:

Thennnn down flew the door,
There was Mary, Mick and Michael O'Flannigan.
They wanted ter know the reason whyyyyyyy
They hadn't been axed to the spreeeeeeee.

As Shamus arrived back at A, a creature stepped out of a bush thumbing a lift. It was McQuonk again.

'I seen enough of A,' he said, climbing into the cab. 'I'd like ter see B again.' Shamus slipped the tractor into gear. 'I didn't tink much of A,' said McQuonk. 'I don't know what people see in it. You sure dere aren't any places called C D or E?'

Shamus was positive. 'You see, Jasper, der term A to B goes for *any* place. For instance, A could be London and B could be Dublin.'

'B is like Dublin?'

'Yes.'

They rode on till they reached B again.

'Let me off here, Shamus,' said McQuonk again, leaping from the cab like a parachutist. 'Tanks,' he said, watching the gull-shrouded tractor drive back to A.

Shamus sang on:

> O'Connor the piper was winkin' an' stinkin'
> While Paddy O'Malley was drinkin'
> At the christening of Danny me boyyyyyyy!

As he arrived back at B, a figure stepped from the bushes thumbing a lift. It was Jasper McQuonk.

'I tell you, Shamus, it's a lie. B is nutting like Dublin,' he said. 'If you must know, it's exactly like A.'

Shamus stopped the tractor. 'Look here, B isn't meant to *look* like Dublin, that's just a figure of speech.' So saying, he started the tractor again. Why did he give this idiot a lift?

'Did I tell you I knew how to eat potatoes?' said McQuonk.

Yes, he had.

Halfway down the field, 'Stop here,' said McQuonk.

Shamus applied the brakes. Now what?

'If dat is A and the other end is B, what letter is dis middle bit?'

For God's sake, this was getting silly. 'Well,' said Shamus, trying to get off the hook, 'well, you could say the Irish Sea.'

'Yes, I can say dat,' said McQuonk. 'The Irish . . . letter C.'

'No no no, man, not the letter C, the word sea – like the ocean.'

'Ahhh, der sea, S E E.'

'Yes.'

'Den I'll get off here.' Again he leapt off into space, landing with a heavy thud. The tractor trundled on amid a

182

symphony of flitter-fluttering gulls. McQuonk observed the birds plundering the earthworm. By Gor, *he* could do that, if a gull could find a worm so could he. He walked to the furrows. Yes! there was a worm, he'd pretend he hadn't seen it. Looking up in the sky, he hummed a little indifferent tune, then, when he thought the worm wasn't watching, he gave a loud 'Hoi ho hupla!!!' Whipping off his trilby, he placed it over the worm. 'Gottcha,' he triumphed. Carefully he slid his hand under the hat: No good, struggling worm, you got to be really clever to escape Jasper McQuonk. By the time Shamus returned, Jasper had a pocket full of them. Climbing up into the cab, he grinned at the world, he'd had a good morning, he'd been to A and B and the Irish Sea. 'Would you like to see a worm, Shamus?'

'Did youse say worm?'

'Yes, would you like to see a worm?'

'No tanks,' said Shamus.

'I got plenty here, Shamus.' He opened his handkerchief, a mass of mud-filled wiggles.

'No tanks. I don't want to see a worm.'

'De're free, I won't miss a couple, you can have –'

'No no no,' interrupted Shamus. Why, why *did* he give him a lift . . . ?

THE HUNT BALLS II

The costumed guests, smashed on Mrs Fitts' punch, assembled in the courtyard to mount their hacks. Napoleon had an identity crisis: '*Zieg Heil!*' he shouted. With some effort they were all trying to mount; some fell off, others balanced precariously. 'Tally-ho-hic-ho,' said Julius Caesar, his laurel crown around his neck. 'Woah,' said Lord Horatio Nelson, hopping madly, one foot in the stirrup as the horse revolved. Thomas à Becket was shouting, 'Keep still, you bastard.' 'Whoopee!' shrieked Saint Theresa of the Little Flower as she hoisted up her habit to reveal black stockings and plump pink throbbing things. '*Nosdrovia*,' said the Czar of Russia, downing a stirrup cup, rearing his horse and sliding down on his proletariat. Marie-Antoinette and Lawrence of Arabia vigorously mounted the same horse from opposite directions colliding in the middle. Sherlock Holmes had done better, he had mounted but back to front. 'Elementary, my dear Hudson,' he said dribbling his stirrup cup down his riding stock, while James Bond in a moment of cinematic bravura vaulted his horse from the rear catching them on the back of the saddle and was now rolling on the ground clutching them, shaken but nut-stirred. A gay Groucho Marx was riding side-saddle. 'Who wants a legover at my time of life, and anyway, if I had a leg over, I'd enter for a three-legged race alone.'

From a flaming master brand they ignited their torches. Clutching a blow-up rubber doll, Hunt Leader St Francis of Assisi signalled 'Follow me', and galloped straight into a stable. Master of the Hounds Scott of the Antarctic blasted his hunting horn and the crowd galloped out of the yard amid confused baying hounds.

A mile ahead, in narcoleptic darkness, ran their quarry in the shape of Jasper McQuonk in his aniseed- and paraffin-soaked trousers. In great uncoordinated thudding leaps he was crossing the Drool countryside leaving a trail of BO and reeking socks. If he was not caught he had been promised a pound and his trousers dry-cleaned free. Just think, he thunk, a whole pound!

Money for jam! he thunked again as he swam a bone-chilling stream, shrivelling them up. Pulling himself up the bank, he could hear the distant cacophony of his pursuers. It gave him new strength, he sped through a hedge colliding with a shepherd at 200 to 1 coming from the other way clutching a shotgun and giving off dog whistles.

'Arrahhh!' said the shepherd. 'Has youse seen a sheep and dog go dis way?'

'No,' said McQuonk, and sped on the wrong way swimming the ice-cold stream again, re-shrivelling them. Listening, he realised he was on the same side as his pursuers, so dived back and recrossed. With water running round his frozen swonnicles, he realised that the hunt was getting louder, that or it was getting nearer. If they were getting louder *and* nearer, that meant they were getting closer than louder and nearer. With icicles hanging from his nose, he made off in the direction of further away. The shepherd who had collided with him in the bush at 200 to 1 now had the scent of aniseed and paraffin on his trousers, which confused the pursuing hounds who split into two groups.

After a while, the pack-leader Webster smelt the trail of a cat that was ensconced in the back garden of Mrs Delores Fruit, the Drool spiritualist person. The moggie shot back in through the cat flap and with a yeowl landed on the top of Mrs Fruit's bedroom cupboard interrupting a masked man singing to Mrs Fruit at pistol point. As the hounds burst into the room, he discharged his pistol into the ceiling bringing plaster down on the already terrified woman. As if that wasn't bad enough, the woman, a victim of alopecia, forgot her wig and ran bald and screaming into the kitchen to phone the police only to find Julius Caesar on a horse at the back door clutching a stock whip.

'What in God's name . . .' she began. Oh! but this was

wonderful – there *was* life after death. 'Are you an ectoplasm?' she said.

Caesar charged up the stairs and came down with the pack. 'Sorry about this, madam.' He placed a pound on the table. 'The Drool Hunt apologise, and your cat is dead.' He strode outside. 'Heel!' he shouted at the baying pack, cracked his whip and caught his earhole. Clutching it, he mounted and drove off with the hounds. 'Beware the Ides of March!' Mrs Fruit shouted ecstatically after him.

A mile away the 200-to-1 shepherd wondered what he was doing up a tree with a pack of rampaging hounds at the bottom, his bottom. Scott of the Antarctic was trying to call them off, blowing his horn so hard he smashed his dentures which flew out at the next jump. What broke the shepherd's heart was seeing his dog Boy race under the tree chasing a flock of sheep, and now he could smell fried eggs.

Still toothless, Scott of the Antarctic blew his horn making futile attempts to control the hounds. In the dark, mistaking the 200-to-1 shepherd for McQuonk, Scott shouted, 'For God's sake, don't come down, they'll tear you to pieces, throw your trousers down. It's your only chance!'

The trousers duly fell amid the dogs who shredded the garment leaving the 200 to 1 shepherd up the tree naked from the waist down. Marie-Antoinette looked up and saw his collection. 'Ohh, just look at those jewels,' she said, hurriedly taking a Polaroid.

'Give me that camera,' raged the shepherd.

Picking up the remains of the trousers, Scott of the Antarctic galloped away followed by the pack of doggies.

Further still, a poacher's trap had closed on McQuonk's boot. It clamped on the sole, and the pack were now one dead cat and a pair of trousers nearer, louder and closer. Frantically he unlaced his boot and withdrew his foot. With this imbalance he sped off but kept veering to the right.

The lead doggie reached the trap, sniffed the boot and fainted. Tarzan hoisted him up across the saddle and the chase continued.

Still veering in a circle, McQuonk came across a poacher's

186

trap with an empty boot in, was this a coincidence? No, it was an empty trap with a boot in. What a bit of luck! Putting his foot in, he laced it up and clumped off with the trap attached to it. This made him veer to the left. The hunt were closing in. He wasn't stupid, he took off *his* trousers and threw them into the river. That'll put 'em off! Mind you, his were nearly off already.

Galloping at speed under a tree, the gay Groucho Marx was dislodged by a low branch. He swung there momentarily, long enough to say, 'Are you the Nat West? They've got branches everywhere.' Then he fell off into the lap of the oncoming James Bond, only to squash his balls yet again. 'Just dropped in for a chat,' said the gay Groucho, waggling his eyebrows. 'My horse has just gone on ahead, normally he goes on legs. Up to now it's been a stable relationship. He got the bit between his teeth, if I had a bit between my teeth I'd give up muff diving.'

Behind came a loud clunk. 'Ow, my fucking head,' shouted St Francis of Assisi, clutching his tonsured wig now rising on a lump.

From a church tower a barn owl called Norrington le Blench watched as the flaming brands disappeared across the fields, gradually homing together.

Ever-vigilant, young Garda Lynch, fresh from his nocturnal window-cleaner report, was patrolling the night streets of Drool. He could hear the sound of a one-legged man with a metal limb running up the high street, but a street light revealed a two-legged man with a trap on one leg and no trousers!

'Stop in the name of the law!' said Lynch, although he didn't know the name of the law.

McQuonk stopped.

'Jasper McQuonk, I'm arresting you for indecent exposure,' said Lynch.

At the police station McQuonk seized his opportunity. Snatching Lynch's truncheon, he walloped him over the head, borrowed his trousers, and ran into the night. No one would stop him getting that pound and the big time.

*

Captain Myles Rafferty was baffled. Twenty years as a fishing-boat skipper, but what was a pack of hounds doing a mile out to sea with a toothless Scott of the Antarctic on a horse, blowing a horn, now all tangled up in the fishing nets? Cursing, the crew drew them aboard amid a mixture of flounder, skate, herrings, mackerel, dogs, horse and Scott of, now, the Atlantic.

From a cupboard on the Castle battlements, Lord O'Gold-stein shouted down to Looney, 'When the hunt returns, set off the fireworks.'

A moment later, wielding a firebrand, the black Quasi-modo shouted, 'They're coming, they're coming to take my Esmerelda.'

Immediately, Looney and the tinker let off a dozen rockets from bottles. Looney watched as they carved golden sabres of light in the night and exploded in clusters, at which moment the returning crazed hunt turned and galloped into the yard.

Seeing St Theresa's bulging thighs Quasimodo cried, 'Esmerelda,' and slid down the rope from the battlement and to the smell of more burning hairs landed at her feet.

'Keep the bugger away!' she shrieked, pushing him away with her foot.

Quasi fell back, hurling his firebrand into the midst of the heaped fireworks. There was a pause as Quasimodo scampered free, then the whole pile ignited. There followed explosion after explosion of fireworks, hundreds of rockets took off at every angle, whoosh! They went through doors, into open windows, even crashing through closed ones, smashing into stables, chicken runs, pigeon lofts, up skirts, horses' noses.

All ran screaming as Roman Candles exploded, Catherine Wheels ran amok sizzling between people's legs, dogs, cats. Jumping Jacks racketed like machine-guns around panic-stricken feet, sparklers blazed with candescent light, big bangers exploded, one under the arse of Quasimodo who was now climbing up the rope to escape. 'The villains are coming!' he shouted above the cacophony of men shouting, horses neighing, hounds barking, chickens clucking, women screaming. In the background, Mrs Fitts' gramophone ground out a ragtime tune. 'My castle, my castle!' wailed Lord O'Goldstein from his cupboard on the battlements, the fire now starting to scorch and blister the wood of the courtyard buildings.

Lucretia Borgia leapt as a firework burst between her legs. 'Darling,' she said.

'Someone call the fire brigade!' shouted the toothless, sea-soaked, stinking-of-flounder Scott of the Antarctic and Atlantic as he and his fish-oiled doggies galloped into the yard. In a frenzy, Looney dialled Emergency.

A flock of sheep galloped through the yard, followed by a dog and a now 300-to-1 trouserless shepherd. The noise and the conflagration had driven all the hounds into adjacent meadows, where they bayed in unison. Lord Nelson organised a bucket chain hurling water into the inferno, from Caesar to St Francis to Tarzan to James Bond to Jasper McQuonk, who threw it all over Nelson.

James Bond had joined the garden hose to the kitchen tap and run at speed to the flames. By the time he'd reached the other end, Jasper McQuonk had disconnected it to fill a bucket. Bond started to run back, by which time McQuonk had reconnected it again; he and his bucket collided with Bond, showering the secret agent. Checking that the hose was connected, he returned to the end as McQuonk disconnected it again to fill his bucket.

From the battlements, the crazed Quasimodo shouted, 'You'll never get her!' and threw a bucket of water down, drenching Bond for the second time. Bond looked into the hose to see if it was blocked. At that moment, McQuonk reconnected it and Bond got it full in his 009 face.

McTruss awoke with a Roman Candle burning his bed, smoke-blackened and scorched. He rushed downstairs to be photographed in front of the inferno, every clue counted. Someone was trying to burn the castle down to destroy the fingerprints!

The horse bales of fodder had ignited. The stable boys

raced all the great fillies out neighing, prancing, whinnying to the safety of the fields. Waiting was the great stallion Sherbert. In twenty minutes he had covered the lot of them and lay down to rest. Oh, what a great life, he thought, who wants to run races?

Aroused by the noise, the Drool villagers stood at a safe distance. ' 'Tis a fine fire,' said one.

O'Brien the phantom singer arrived, an opportunity! 'Don't panic!' he called, standing on a chair and starting to sing. 'Beeeee my loveeeeeeeeeeeeeeeeeee, and with your Kissessssssssssssssss set me burning.' A bucketful from Quasi-modo landed on him. Spluttering but undaunted, he sang on until he was lifted off the chair by a combined Giant Rocket and a Whizz-Bang. His trousers smouldering, he remounted the chair. 'One kiss is all that I'm asking forrrrrrrrrr.'

Back at Drool police station, Sergeant Kelly found Lynch unconscious on the floor with no trousers and only one boot.

Back at the fire, O'Brien stopped singing. Who's this with a plaster on his leg? Prune! He'd get him! Like a miracle it started to rain. A groan of disappointment went up from the spectators.

Up the road raced the Limerick fire brigade. As the first spots fell, the fire chief prayed, 'Please God, don't let it go out before we get there.' They entered the gates – thank God it was still burning. Some of the spectators threw themselves in front of the engine. 'Spoilsports!' they shouted.

O'Brien pounced on Prune. 'Rory Prune, I arrest you for the –' He got no further. The fire engine knocked him down. As the first hose gushed on, Father Costello arrived on his bike. Shouting above the noise, he prayed, 'Dear Lord, bless this fire and all the dear loved ones departed. Bless the firemen, bless their hoses and the brass attachments. Oh, yes, bless their water, and may the insurance company pay up promptly and God forgive Ian Paisley for doing all this.'

In the field, the torrential rain was washing the black and white dye off Sherbert. At one stage one side looked like a Zebra and the other like a batik abstract.

On the smoke-blackened terrace, McQuonk in Garda

190

Lynch's trousers and one boot had cornered Lord O'Goldstein being massaged by Mrs Fitts in time to a tango record. 'Dey didn't catch me,' chortled McQuonk, 'so you owe me.'

Sobbing, Lord O'Goldstein, now dressed as Marlene Dietrich in *The Blue Angel*, led McQuonk through bursting fireworks to his bedroom and felt under the mattress. 'How much?' he sobbed.

'One pound,' said Jasper.

'Ohhhhhh!' groaned O'Goldstein, as he withdrew a pound. 'Here, but first sign this receipt for five.'

What luck! thought McQuonk, a whole pound and a receipt for five, making a total of six pounds!

Fearing for its welfare, Mick Looney ran and located his horse. But wait!! Great gollops of green gunk! Great streams of stingling stonk! It was now brown . . . BROWN!!! Like a public toilet, the penny dropped. It was Sherbert! And *four* legs. He'd found more of the horse than was advertised. A tousand pounds! Rich! Rich! Rich! He grabbed the halter at the very moment a Whizz-Bang exploded under the horse's tail. With a great leap, it galloped off round the field dragging the luckless Looney through a mixture of sheep, horse and cow dung.

A dreary dawn broke over the smouldering burnt-out wing of the castle, the whole area was a sodden swamp of dead fireworks, slurry, mud and discarded historical costumes. Inside the castle, tired out by a night's firefighting and fucking, the guests slumbered in their or somebody else's beds.

The occasion had been an absolute boon to the *Drool Bugle*. All through the night Mr McGuinness slaved at the compositor's set preparing the morning edition.

TterribuL @ ? FIRE WREX WINg of/3 CASTLe%.
LONDon PROP/ERTY DevolOPER FINS SHE@RBERTT.

Drool, Tuẽsdee

List niGht, dewring a FeerWok partee, t he StaBle wingg cort back fyre. Millions ½ of pounds wirth of dimige WAs done to thE value of twenty pounds o n o.Dewering the fire Mr Looney disco-vered the missUNG Sherber(t,he will will WILL, receiv?e atho-usend ponds reward. Our said no oneeee wa' hurt. Clicks go won hourto-Onight During the fire Garda O'Brien Hel/ped 2 pot it out @ by sinGING

(Reuter)

THE CEREMONY

The great reward ceremony was taking place outside the Drool council office and launderette. A small wooden rostrum had been draped with the Irish tricolour and, because of the shortage, the flags of the United Arab Emirates, Malta and Uganda. The ceremony with the Drool Girl Pipers playing 'A Nation Once Again', again and again and again. Along with the village dignitaries, Lord Mayor James Duffy mounted the rostrum, a mite too small. They all stood huddled together like penguins in a blizzard.

Looney himself stood among the massed spectators, all awaiting the spectacle. The Gardai Lynch, O'Brien and Sergeant Kelly held back the crowd of fifteen. The ceremony continued with the late arrival of Father Costello on a bike. From the middle of the high street he gave the blessing: 'God bless the Lord Mayor and the dignitaries, God bless the rostrum, God bless the pipers, God bless the bagpipes, God bless the lead piper with big tits. God bless the reward of one thousand pounds less tax –' He was cut short as the morning Limerick commuter bus thundered by, splattering him in mud and driving him into the gutter, which he blessed.

Without waiting, Inspector McTruss opened the proceedings: 'Mister Lord Mayor, ladies and g –' The mike went dead. He continued like a silent film mouthing words.

'We can't hear you, mister,' called a voice.

McTruss banged the microphone on the floor. To cover the embarrassed silence, the pipe band struck up 'A Nation Once Again' and again and again. At the moment the mike came on McTruss had to stand and wait. The pipes droned to silence.

'Hello, testing testing,' said McTruss. 'Ladies and gentlemen, his worship the Lord Mayor . . .'

The crowd applauded. 'What about my sister, yer bastard!' said a voice.

James Duffy forced a sickly grin on to an already sickly face. 'Ladies and gentlemen, may I remind you that my wife Mave's outsize clothing shop is open until six o'clock. Now, as you know, Sherbert has been found safe and one leg more than expected. First, I must thank the efforts of the Drool Gardai and Inspector McTruss . . .'

The crowd applauded. 'What about my sister, yer bastard!' said the voice.

Duffy donned his glasses. 'Now, I have great pleasure of presenting one thousand pounds' reward to the man who found Sherbert, his name is' – here he referred to a piece of paper – 'three pounds of potatoes, a small brown loaf and' he paused – 'I'm sorry, ladies and gentlemen' – he turned the paper over –

'You focked her, didn't you?' said the voice.

The sickly grin returned to Duffy's guilty face. 'His name is Mr and Mrs Dick Looney.'

From the crowd stepped Mr and Mrs Dick Looney, only to have his way blocked by a white Mercedes pulling up. It was crammed with chattering Japanese tourists.

'Preese,' said the Nip driver, 'preese, this way to Drublin?'

'Yes,' said Looney.

Looney mounted the rostrum and shook hands with Duffy, who handed him a thousand pounds less his commission for the occasion, plus his business card, 'Financial Investments & Second-Hand Car Dealer'. Looney took the mike which now gave off a high-pitched heterodyne whistle.

From the back came a running sixteen-stone electrician Len Murtagh. He leapt on to the rostrum. There came a splintering sound as the rostrum collapsed. From the mixture of screams, groans, coughs, planks of wood, chairs and dust, the victims extricated themselves. McTruss took photographs, every clue counted. Father Costello blessed the accident. O'Brien ran forward, grabbing a chair. He stood on it and said, 'Don't panic,' then sang 'Be my love'. The white Mercedes returned, the driver shouted at Looney, 'You

194

brasted! You bruddy riar! That not the way to Drublin,' and drove off. Father Costello blessed the departing Nips. The mike restored, standing in the ruins of the rostrum, Duffy called for three cheers. The pipe band struck up 'A Nation Once Again' again and again. The occasion ended on a familiar note:

'What about my sister, yer bastard!'

THE MONEY

Yes! The money, the thousand pounds of money, he was now a thousand-pound millionaire. It had been handed to himself in one pound notes stuffed into a small canvas zip bag. Back at the cottage, he tried to open it but the zip stuck. Again and again he tried to pull it open, and again and again it didn't. He'd have to get that money out soon before it lost its value. As long as the zip remained stuck the thousand pounds belonged to the bag, leaving him penniless. Using a bread knife, he cut a hole in the floor of the bag, oh yes, no canvas bag was going to make a bloody fool of him. Carefully he extricated the trapped money, he took it out in crumpled handfuls, patiently he straightened out the notes, laying them side by side on his bed. When he had filled that he continued to lay them out on the dining table then the sideboard, the mantelpiece, the washstand, finally the window ledges. Then he laboriously started to count them individually in a loud voice.

ONE! So far so good. Using all his powers of concentration, in five minutes he had got up to twelve, at which moment Mrs Looney came through the front door along with a Force Nine gale. In one great gust the room swirled with the reward money. With a maniacal scream Looney clawed burning notes from the fire. All his life he wanted money to burn and here it was happening!

'Youse bloody fool, woman!' he yelled. 'Look wot youse done!'

Mrs Looney *was* looking at what she had done. 'Wot do youse expect me to do, come down the bloody chimney?'

Yes, she should have come down the bloody chimney! It was true, then, money didn't always bring happiness.

It took him half an hour to lay the money out again. Oh! it looked beautiful. He stood back to admire it, he went out the back door and looked at it through the window, he came in again and walked around the bed and the table muttering 'Lubbley, lubbley' – a poor substitute for 'Lovely, lovely'. He looked in the mirror and saw the thousand pounds reflected, making him *twice* as rich. Fancy, just by looking in a mirror, you could double your money! But mirrors are very unreliable, the moment he looked away the money vanished.

Father Costello and the gale came in, and when Looney had collected it all again and stopped swearing Father Costello blessed the money. Looney gave him five burnt pounds for the poor of the parish, which just happened to be Father Costello.

Again Looney was swearing and pound notes swirling as the Force Nine gale returned with Inspector McTruss. When Looney had finished telling him he should have 'come down the fockin' chimney', he congratulated Looney on finding Sherbert with four legs instead of three. 'Annuder day and *I'd* ha' found him meself,' he said as he was photographed with Looney and the money.

'The case is now closed,' said McTruss.

'Yes, dat's because the bloody zip was stuck,' said Looney. 'Now, gentlemen, if youse will excuse me I gotta count der money to see if it's all there.' Most certainly Looney wasn't all there. 'I'll see youse all at the pub fer a celebration dis evening.'

The two men departed leaving Looney counting the money. Just wait till they saw this roll at the pub.

By ten-thirty that night Looney and the entire town were pissed and broke.

The search for his royal blood had not borne fruit. It had not borne fish, chips, fowl or bacon, it had borne onion-flavoured crisps, Mars bars, Big Macs and nearer Dublin a Chinese takeaway. What he wanted was an Irish takeaway kingship and a win on Littlewoods.

The holiday in dreary Drool ended and the lost Looneys returned to 113b Ethel Road, the family seat. They arrived back in dark, dank, dreary Kilburn night through the unlit hall into the kitchen where they gratefully dumped their luggage. Mrs Looney automatically put the kettle on. Looney himself walked wearily to the parlour to see in the darkened room the outline of his Gothic throne chair occasionally lit up by the light of a passing bus. How sad, he had hoped to have returned and sat in that chair as a King of Ireland. With a strain and a groan he lit the gas fire then sat on his throne, silent in the dark, the only sound the hiss of the gas fire and the swish of traffic passing in the rain-coated streets.

Looney sat staring into the gas fire's hypnotic flames, his mind wandered into fields of lost opportunities where, lost in Tara's green shadow long-forgotten, Irish high kings lay buried in their gilded finery: the glint of greeny-gold crowns on yellow skulls; Ossian fingers fallow-gripping the La Tène filagreed sword hilts. On once-breathing breasts now fallen, bones pressed giant battle shields: burnished copper bosses green with the finger of time; inlays of molten red, purple and yellow glasses glimmered through dust. Above lay what once adorned a high king's throat, the sweeping golden lanula, and by his side a silver Ardagh chalice in whose bowl once flowed some savage fiery opiate that inspired Ougham to write poems of horsemen passing by with the bark of wolfhounds in their flying heels. Here, then, could be lying in time-locked silence King Niall of the nine hostages, or even Cuchulain himself. All above could be their tuatha where first came the ancient red-haired, green-eyed Ciuithni. Now gone were their gods, gone their harp-borne songs, gone their fires, gone their dreams, yet, still, the wind howled over Maughan Hill . . . Tomorrow, Looney would put an ad in the *Exchange Mart & Gazette*: For Sale, one throne-like chair. £3. o.n.o.